The
Enduring Curiosity
of
Mitsy Howard

Also by this author

14 Viney Hill
TravelWorks
HomeWorks
Oh, and another thing...

The
Enduring Curiosity
of
Mitsy Howard

- A Walk in the Mill -

Carole Susan Smith

Copyright © 2020 Carole Susan Smith

ISBN: 9798648634251

PublishNation
www.publishnation.co.uk

This work of fiction is dedicated to all carers, especially those who work in residential homes, nursing homes and retirement homes, in recognition of their service to individuals and the community.

About the Author

The opportunity to do many unusual things and to work in other countries including Siberia, the Palestinian Occupied Territories, the Far East, across Europe as well as in the UK, provided the source for Carole's three light-hearted memoirs. She has worked in education, health and social care as well as other industry sectors. The inspiration for her subsequent two novels, *14 Viney Hill* and *The Enduring Curiosity of Mitsy Howard – A Walk in the Mill* - has been solely her overactive imagination.

Part I

How Mitsy settles into her new home and has adventures

"Is it true that someone saw a ghost last week?" asked the very tall, white haired man to the people sitting at the breakfast table. Everyone looked at everyone else and when no response was forthcoming, they all returned to their conversations as if nothing had punctured the gentle murmur of early morning voices.

Mitsy looked at the man. From his bearing and the way that he posed his question so confidently, she guessed he had been in a senior position when he was at work. She could imagine him standing at the head of a large table in a Boardroom somewhere, commanding attention. Tentatively, very tentatively, she raised her hand in line with her shoulder until she caught his eye and nodded.

The man got to his feet and walked round to the empty seat next to Mitsy, indicating with his head whether he might join her. "How exciting! Do tell me all about it!" he exclaimed, as he tucked his rather long, ungainly legs under the table.

"Well, I'm not really sure…" began Mitsy as her fellow diners left the table and slowly headed off to their rooms. "You see, I'm not a very good sleeper. Actually, I'm awake most nights until the early hours. I get bored lying in bed not sleeping, so last Wednesday I walked along the corridor to see if anyone else was awake and who was in the kitchen as I fancied a cup of tea."

The man smiled, "I think a full night's sleep eludes most of us as we get older. I'm Arthur by the way." He held out his hand in a very polite manner and Mitsy shook it gently, while continuing her story.

"I didn't switch any lights on, as the street lamps are so bright that it wasn't necessary. Just as I turned the corner there was a woman standing at the bottom of the big staircase. You know, the stairs that go up to Mr and Mrs P's apartment?" she asked.

Arthur nodded as if he knew where she was describing, so she carried on with her story.

"Well, the woman seemed to be wearing a long, white nightdress. She had dark wavy hair which hung down almost to her waist. She was quite young and pretty. I thought perhaps she was a young relative of Mr and Mrs Podsiadlo, so I called out: 'Hello! Are you after a cuppa too?'"

"The woman smiled back at me but then as I approached her, she vanished!"

Arthur's face lit up. "What do you mean - she vanished?"

"Well," said Mitsy, "she just wasn't there any more. She sort-of dissolved. I cannot describe it any better than that."

"Weren't you frightened?" he asked with concern.

"No. I really wasn't. She seemed so real and it was such a friendly smile. Anyway, Maggie was in the kitchen so she made me a cup of tea and I told her about it. Maggie said they had often wondered if there was a ghost here as there had been stories, but as no-one had seen anything for years, they assumed it was either a fanciful anecdote or the ghost had gone away. She also said I probably shouldn't talk about it to the other residents because it might frighten some of the more nervous ones."

2

Sally was clearing the breakfast table meanwhile, and to say she was making a bit of a clatter was an understatement. Her less than subtle behaviour suggested she really wanted Mitsy and Arthur out of the way.

Arthur appeared not to notice Sally, and continued to chat to Mitsy while the other residents left the room.

"Did you know that early in 1916, Appledore House became a Red Cross Hospital? It was used as a centre for caring for the sick and wounded British troops during the Great War. I've been reading up about it."

"How interesting," said Mitsy.

"If you'd like to know more of the history of this place, I'd be happy to share my findings with you. This is partly why I was interested in the ghost," said Arthur. "Would you like to come out for lunch one day? We could go to the pub up the road. I haven't been there yet and it would be pleasant to have company."

This was not exactly what Mitsy was expecting but she found herself agreeing to meet at twelve noon the next day, for an excursion with Arthur. I hardly know the man, she said to herself but I suppose it cannot do any harm.

2

When she arrived in the hallway, Arthur was already standing by the front door. "I understand that we have to hang our room keys on the hooks here, to show that we are out," said Arthur.

"Yes. It's just a security thing. It's like they used to do in old-fashioned hotels in the days before we had key cards. Personally, I cannot quite get used to having to ring the doorbell to get back indoors but I suppose they have got to be careful if there are any residents prone to go walkabout! I've told the kitchen we shall both be out this lunchtime; I hope that was in order, Arthur?"

Arthur smiled as he took her arm and they walked across the large gravelled parking area together, turning right in the direction of the public house.

"So how long have you lived at Appledore House, Misty?"

"Oh. Actually, my name is Mitsy..."

"My mistake. I do apologise. Mitsy is rather unusual," said Arthur.

"Ha-ha! You are not the first to be confused! I grew up in the war years but my parents were a bit New Age before it was even a 'thing'; they were not exactly travellers but they did live in a caravan and had quite a bohemian lifestyle until we children came along. My elder brother was called Rock, my sister is called Sky and I was going to be called Misty. When Dad got to the Registrar's office, we think perhaps he had had too much to drink because he didn't spell my name correctly. I've been happy to keep Mitsy, although it can be a bit inconvenient sometimes."

They walked along in companionable silence for a while, until Mitsy remembered that she had been asked a question.

"I've been at Appledore House for nearly three months. I wouldn't say I'm feeling at home yet, but mostly it's OK. I think after a lifetime of being independent and largely self-sufficient it is quite difficult to live in a community with everything being done for you. Mind you, I don't miss the housework, the washing and ironing, the cleaning, the gardening, the shopping and all the work involved in preparing endless meals for one!" Then she took a deep breath. "Arthur, I've done nothing but talk about myself. Sorry about that, please tell me how you are settling in."

At this point they approached the front door of the Standsfield Arms, an impressive-looking traditional hostelry. Arthur courteously stood to one side at the doorstep so that Mitsy could enter the lounge bar. Oak beams, a blazing fire and a cheerful welcome from the landlady set the scene for a relaxing lunch. Mitsy asked for a glass of white wine while Arthur cheerfully ordered a locally brewed beer. By the time they were settled into comfortable chairs they had both decided on a ploughman's lunch. Mitsy noticed privately that there was no attempt at political correctness here 'it's a ploughman's lunch and we'll have no truck with plough person's here!' she imagined someone saying.

"Yes, thank you," said Arthur. "I am beginning to settle in. This is only my second week. My home is in Huddersfield where I lived with my wife Ivy. Ivy passed away last Christmas after a short illness. She had pneumonia."

"I'm sorry to hear that, Arthur. You must miss her dreadfully."

"I thought I was doing alright on my own but rather clumsily I tripped on the pavement outside my house and ended up in hospital. Bruises and broken bones heal eventually but somehow, I didn't feel like going back. My daughters tried to get me to move down south to be near them. They both live in London; Jackie has a flat in North London and Marie and her husband Alan live south of the river. You can imagine that whichever one I agreed to go to, it would upset the other! I didn't really fancy living in London, it's a young person's city I think."

Mitsy smiled privately at that assumption but nodded sympathetically to Arthur.

"So, you came to Appledore House! What was London's loss was our gain!"

Oh dear, she thought. I'm in danger of appearing to flirt when all I really wanted to do was to put the man at ease. I'd better take it easy with the wine.

Fortunately, two ploughman's lunches arrived and they both exclaimed at the selection of ham, cheese – Wensleydale of course – pickles and home baked bread. There was so much on their plates that they both feared they wouldn't be able to do justice to the meal.

A large, black Labrador ambled slowly into the room. Mitsy gave him a friendly pat on the head as he stretched himself out on the rug in front of the fire. After a few minutes a member of staff came running in: "Peter, you bad boy. You mustn't come in here when people are eating."

Both Arthur and Mitsy assured her that Peter was welcome to share their fire and neither was concerned to have the pub dog for company.

"I should explain what's amusing me," said Mitsy. "My husband's name was Peter. And my son is Pete also. I'm not sure I've met a Peter dog before!"

"How long have you been on your own then?" asked Arthur.

Mitsy thought it was quite a strange way to phrase the question and to be honest, she would have preferred the conversation to concentrate on the ghost sighting rather than personal matters.

"That's difficult to answer because my Peter was a Petty Officer in the Royal Navy and he was away at sea frequently during our long and happy marriage." She didn't want to be too obvious but felt it was time to return to the ostensible reason for Arthur's lunch invitation.

"Anyway, do tell me what you have discovered about Appledore House please."

In between eating lunch and offering another small glass of wine which was declined, Arthur described some of the history of their residential home. It seemed to be his way of getting familiar with what was to be his new abode.

Mitsy was able to add an update to this, which included how Mr and Mrs Podsiadlo came to own and run Appledore House. The young couple were very fortunate to take over the care home for a modest outlay, when as a business it was not exactly thriving. They had both worked extremely hard ever since to turn it into a going concern. The residents affectionately called them Mr and Mrs P, although Mitsy had her doubts whether this was just friendly or because people couldn't pronounce their Polish surname! At the beginning Mr P did all the property maintenance and as Mrs P was a qualified nurse, she took charge of everything that was to do with the residents. These days they were semi-retired and lived 'above the shop' while a reliable team of staff basically ran everything on a day to day basis.

The warmth of the fire, the friendliness of the staff, the food and the alcohol all contributed to a relaxed atmosphere at the Standsfield Arms and the couple were happy to tell each other just a little of their lives before moving to Appledore House.

Arthur was intrigued to discover that Mitsy was an experienced heritage researcher. That was not how Mitsy explained it but rather "I dabble a bit on the internet as I'm interested in family history." It was one of the ways in which she had learned to occupy herself since her husband Peter died.

After their now empty plates had been cleared and coffee had been consumed, there seemed no reason to prolong the lunch outing. Ever the diplomat, Mitsy observed that she had probably be better getting back as she had a number of important emails to deal with.

Their stroll back took barely ten minutes, although Mitsy helpfully used the time to tell Arthur about the outings organised by the Home, as well as the weekly activities that he might wish to join in on. She was rather wary of becoming his only friend and thought it would be advisable if he widened his circle sooner rather than later.

"Thank you, Arthur. That was a lovely lunch and it made a pleasant change to go out. I shall continue to look into the history of this area and I will, of course, tell you of any further ghostly sightings!" she quipped. With that, she picked up her room key and headed off up the corridor before any further plans could be made.

3

Mitsy stood in front of the full-length mirror which was adjacent to her wardrobe. "Not bad for nearly 79," she murmured to herself. Mitsy was, indeed, still a good-looking woman and many would have thought she was at least ten or fifteen years younger. Her hair had turned to an attractive shade of steel grey, which was now its natural colour, and she was thankful to have avoided what she considered the distressful experience of her mousey-blonde locks fading to yellowish-white. She made an effort to have her hair cut regularly but this was something she had not completely resolved in her new home. There was a hairdresser's salon in the parade of shops nearby, which she tried shortly after moving in, but she really wasn't happy with the outcome. The woman was rather too used to cutting the hair of elderly ladies who wanted a shampoo and set and Mitsy preferred a more modern look. She wondered whether she could find a really good stylist in Bradford who would be willing to call at Appledore House, if she could get a few other residents to join in.

Peering more closely at her face, she noticed that a couple of so-called laughter lines were slightly more prominent. Well, I've done a lot of living and laughing so it's no surprise if my face shows it, she said to herself. She decided she should try to drink more water and get out in the fresh air more regularly.

Completing the appraisal, she ran her arthritic hands down her body. She was of slender build and apart from the gradual thickening of her waist-line, which she had failed to shift since her mid-fifties, she was really in good shape.

Of course, wearing well-cut clothes certainly helped and she had always chosen classic styles and veered towards more expensive dresses, skirts and trousers in the belief that they were an investment.

Her attention was suddenly drawn towards the window. Mr P appeared to be talking to someone in the bushes. She really liked her room as it overlooked the garden on this side and there was a smaller window on the other side giving a view of the road.

She tapped on the window and Mr P stood up suddenly. He waved back and Mitsy could see he had been talking to a large ginger cat. That looks like Puss the Second, but of course it isn't, she sighed to herself.

"Well, this won't do," she said to herself, as she moved towards her writing desk, "it's time to catch up with Pete."

Mitsy had been worried at first that she would feel too cloistered by living in just one room when she moved into Appledore House. As it turned out, she was able to take over a double room that had been vacated by two people so she actually had plenty of space. There was a large bed, a chest of drawers for storage, a double wardrobe, two comfortable chairs in front of the TV, a coffee table and a work desk with chair where her laptop was always open – she really couldn't ask for more. The en suite bathroom was ideal too, with bath, a power shower, toilet and heated towel rail. She hadn't actually used the bath much although it had one of those things that help you get in and out. She thought it was actually better and easier to use than the bathroom at her old home. The room was comfortably warm and if it got too hot, she could always open a window for ventilation. It was number six at the far end of the downstairs corridor.

Dear Pete, I did intend to email you earlier today but, in the event, I went out for lunch with a friend. All is well here and I'm keeping busy with my internet research on the family. When

10

do you think you might get over here? Love
Mum xxx

Mitsy pressed send and then noticed that she had
received an email just a couple of minutes earlier.

Dear Mum I was going to write earlier today
but things are a bit busy at work. I'm coming
over next Thursday so we can sort out the
house. I've booked my flight, a rental car and
the Travelodge so we're all set. Love Pete xxx

Mitsy laughed to think that they had probably been
writing to each other at the same time. Email or Messenger
worked perfectly well for them most of the time and it was
cheaper and more convenient than using the phone.
She couldn't ask for a better son. He was sensible,
hardworking and did everything he could to make sure she
was fine after his dad had passed away. He was fifty-three
so not really a lad any more but sometimes when she
thought of him, she still pictured him in his school uniform
and short trousers.

Hi Pete! Message received and understood.
Looking forward to seeing you! Mum xxx

Of course, she knew they had to sort out the house in
Harrogate. It had been empty since she moved out nearly
three months ago and it was time to tidy things up, dispose
of furniture and put it on the market. She wasn't looking
forward to the task, given that she would be leaving behind
all those memories of her happy childhood and then making
the house their own family home with husband Peter. It had
to be sold because she needed to raise the money to pay her
monthly bill to Appledore House. She tried to think of it as
just like paying rent but it was rather a lot of money as it

11

covered food, laundry and personal care. Mitsy didn't regret the move. As Pete said at the time, it made sense to sort things out while she was still capable. He didn't actually say 'compos mentis' but she was realistic enough to know that many people lose some of their mental faculties as they get older, even if it is no more than being a bit forgetful.

4

The next day, Arthur made a beeline for Mitsy at breakfast. "Any more sightings?" he asked with a glint in his eye. Mitsy smiled, "Nothing yet Arthur. Perhaps I imagined it!" "I've found out some more about the history of Appledore House," he said. "Perhaps we could have lunch again sometime?"

"Well maybe, but that wouldn't be for a while as my son Pete is coming over for a few days. We have quite a lot of business matters to deal with."

She didn't want to crush his enthusiasm but on the other hand she really hoped Arthur would make some new friends.

Lucy, another resident, was half listening to the conversation: "Ooh, that sounds interesting Arthur."

Mitsy took her cue from Lucy and raising her voice just a little above the general murmur of conversation, "Perhaps, Arthur, you could assemble all the information you have on the history of Appledore House and give a little talk for us on your findings? I wouldn't be surprised if some of the staff would like to hear too!"

There were several nods of agreement and Lucy said, "Oh yes please!"

"Will we have a chance to meet your son?" asked Lucy, turning to address her question to Mitsy.

"Probably not; I suppose it depends on what time his flight arrives."

"Oh. Is he travelling far?"

"Not really. He lives in Dublin, so a short flight to Leeds/Bradford airport is nothing compared with his usual

13

work travel." Mitsy was quite a private person and she didn't really want to chatter too much, but somehow, she got led by Lucy's expression of interest into saying more than she intended.

"Pete works for the European Commission so he travels round all of the member states. Don't ask me what he does! He enjoys it anyway."

"So, you must have Irish ancestors Mitsy?" asked another person, as the breakfast table discussion developed.

"Yes. My mother was Irish. Although Pete's lived there for years. When it looked like the UK was going to leave Europe, Pete got Irish citizenship because his granny was Irish, otherwise he wouldn't have had the freedom to travel in order to carry on in the same job."

She felt that this was quite enough information for the assembled group, so she folded her serviette and rose from the table. "Excuse me, I've got lots of things to do today."

Back in room six, Mitsy looked around her room and concluded that she wasn't really sure what to do with all this spare time. She wasn't in the mood for her ancestry search so she flicked through the channels on her television without finding anything on morning TV that appealed to her. Mitsy sighed and turned off the blank screen. Her attention turned to her bookcase, where she had a few reference books, including a dictionary and a thesaurus for when she did the crosswords, as well as quite a collection of paperbacks and a Kindle loaded up with as yet unread fiction.

Her mind was already rather jumpy this morning and she knew if she didn't calm herself, by the evening she would be awake half the night and feeling exhausted the next day. She glanced at the bottom shelf of the bookcase where on moving day she had hurriedly stuffed some photo albums from the days when all family records were printed photographs, embossed on the back with the Kodak logo or similar.

First, she picked up her wedding album. It wasn't labelled as such but it did have a piece of card with *8 June 1963* sellotaped on the spine which, of course, was their special day. Mitsy sat staring at the picture of them both, just outside the church smiling happily and framed by the entrance arch. She well remembered the fuss her parents had made because Mitsy and Peter wanted to get married in a church whereas they wanted to have an informal civic ceremony followed by a party in a field of all things! Thankfully the young couple's preferences prevailed and the church wedding went ahead albeit with rather bad grace. The Big Freeze of 1963, with its long, extremely cold winter had at last come to an end. Mitsy and Peter were so relieved that the sun shone on them that day.

Next to Peter, both looking very smart in their Naval uniforms, stood Robert his Best Man. Mitsy's dress was floor-length cream voile, floaty and romantic. She loved it. She also recalled the arguments she had with her sister Sky who was to be the Matron of Honour and was determined to wear an up-to-the-minute dress with a pinched in waist and a full ballerina-style skirt. It wasn't that she thought Sky would outshine the bride, just that she wanted to co-ordinate how they all looked. Not much chance of that with her parents in any case. In the end, she gave in, as long as the dress was a plain colour and not patterned. In fact, Sky looked lovely in her trendy, pale pink creation which gave a special glow to her auburn hair.

Earlier that year, their brother Rock had died on his motorbike in a terrible road accident. Whilst it would have been easy to blame the slushy, melting snow or the wind and the lashing rain, the truth was that Rock was always reckless and it would seem that a simple error of judgement had caused him to hit the bridge head-on, causing severe injuries from which he never recovered. In the wedding photo, without it being intended, there seemed to be a gap where Rock would have stood.

15

Mr and Mrs Howard senior, Peter's parents, looked on proudly. They had doubts when their son wanted to join the Royal Navy and go to sea but he had certainly grown into a fine young man. They liked Mitsy and had welcomed her into their wider family.

Mitsy's parents, on the other hand, seemed determined to look out of place. Both deeply tanned, bejewelled and dressed in long kaftans recently obtained on their travels, they stuck out like a sore thumb amongst the other guests. Whilst kaftans are fashionable as holiday wear these days, at the time they did look as if they had just arrived from the Asian sub-continent. Mitsy loved her parents dearly but they could be annoying sometimes.

She smiled affectionately; what a lovely wedding day that was. Of course, she and Peter did have difficulties to deal with, as most couples do, but with the benefit of hindsight she was able to reflect on their happiness over many years of marriage and that brought a contented glow to her spirits.

'Right,' said Mitsy aloud, but to herself. 'It's time I carried on with the ancestry search.' She was really looking forward to discovering more about her father's family, although the Irish roots on her mother's side were also intriguing her. These were always known about and it did help Pete to get an Irish passport, but there was so much more to learn. She logged on to the website she generally used for this activity and sighed to find half a dozen 'hints' for her to look at. It seemed she wasted more time checking out their hints and discarding them than making good use of the access to their records.

Before she could get underway, there was a knock at the door. She smiled to herself. She wasn't really in the mood for the painstaking effort the research required, so the interruption was more than welcome.

"Hello, I'm Norma and I've just moved in next door."

"Oh, do come in Norma. Yes, sit over here where there's a view of the garden. I'm Mitsy although I expect you already know that. How are you settling in?"

"I don't know yet," said Norma. "It's all so very different."

"I found, in my first few days here, that it was strange not having things to do, so I have devised some activities to keep me out of mischief! How about you Norma, have you moved from far away?"

At this juncture in the conversation, one of the care staff appeared at the door with a tray of tea and biscuits.

"Thank you, Jo. Do you think we could have another cup and saucer as Norma and I are just getting acquainted?"

Both women were keen to get to know each other but equally nervous not to be seen as nosey. Once the tea had been poured and the biscuits offered, they both began to speak at once. After some embarrassed laughter, "Go ahead Norma, please" said Mitsy.

It transpired that Norma had indeed moved from far away. She had been taken ill while living in Port Elizabeth, South Africa. After she had recovered, her daughter insisted on her moving back to Yorkshire, to be near the family. So, not only had she a new home to settle in to, she also had to adapt to a considerable change in climate.

"Excuse me for asking but you have a really unusual name Mitsy. Does it have a special meaning?" asked Norma.

Mitsy was getting used to explaining her name to virtually everyone she met at Appledore House. She had rehearsed a simple response which she duly trotted out.

"I've no idea if it means anything! The truth is that my parents were prototype hippies before we three children put the brakes on their chilled-out existence and wanderlust. Anyway, when Dad registered my birth, we think he had had a bit too much to drink and instead of writing 'Misty' he muddled the letters up. My sister is called Sky and my

17

brother's name was Rock – at least Dad couldn't mess those up!"

The two women laughed and it augured well for having Norma in the room next door. With Raymond, who was a quiet and courteous gentleman, living on the opposite side of the corridor, Mitsy started to feel more comfortable in her new home already. Some of the other residents had lived at Appledore for a long time and so she was pleased that she would no longer be the newcomer.

When Mitsy's son Pete had suggested that it would be sensible to move out of the large and rambling property she had shared for many years with her much-loved husband and to move into a modern and well-managed care home, she was not at all happy with the prospect. In her head she still felt like a twenty-year-old, totally free and independent. Over time though, she realised that her life consisted of cleaning rooms that she never used and trying to hold in check the endless growth of weeds and shrubs in their once-tidy garden. Appledore Residential Care Home was turning out to be a relief from all that unnecessary and soul-destroying labour and left her with time to do some fun things at last.

Norma stood up, placing her cup and saucer carefully on the coffee table. "Well Mitsy, I'm delighted to have met you and I think I should get on with some of my unpacking now."

Hmm. Not overstaying her welcome either, observed Mitsy to herself, already thinking that she and Norma would get on just fine.

Mitsy and Norma sat next to each other at dinner time and Mitsy introduced her new neighbour to everyone else sitting at their table. The meal was toad in the hole, served with fresh vegetables and steaming, flavoursome gravy. Everyone commented on the lightness of the Yorkshire pudding surrounding the locally produced sausages.

Mitsy privately thought it was all so much better than anything she could have made herself, as peeling vegetables had become impossible with her arthritic hands. In any case, eating alone had lost its appeal for her many years ago; it was good to have some company and then the freedom to go back to one's room, close the door and be private.

5

Mitsy had always been self-sufficient and it was strange for her now that her son Pete had rather taken control, once she had moved into Appledore House. All those years with Peter away at sea meant that she just got on with things until the next time he was on shore leave. Of course, sometimes she was able to accompany him on overseas postings and that had always been an adventure. She had especially enjoyed Valletta in Malta, for the hot, sunny climate and the more relaxed way of life. She missed her home and her friends though, and in some ways, she was quite lonely. The Maltese people were kind and friendly, but because their language was rather alien to her ears – it was quite like Arabic – she mainly had only Peter to talk to in those days.

Thursday morning arrived and she realised that Pete would want to take her to the old house, just to make sure there were no personal items she wanted. They had done a fairly thorough check when she moved out, but this would be the last chance to pick up any mementos. Pete had already declined to take any of the furniture himself. His three-bedroom flat in Dublin was spacious but it was modern and whilst he didn't want to hurt his mother's feelings, there was no way he wanted any of that dingy old, mahogany furniture.

It was mid-morning when Pete tapped on the door of room six. "Are you ready Mum? We've got lots to do today and tomorrow!"

In some ways Mitsy was looking forward to these outings with her son but with mixed feelings as it would be a door on her former life closed permanently, both metaphorically and in practice.

Pete explained as he settled her into the rental car that they had a busy programme of activity. First, they would go to the house and check each room carefully, collecting anything she wanted to keep. He would then take her back to Appledore House. Later, he had an appointment with a man from a house clearance company who would assess the cost of emptying the property and say what he would pay for the furniture he could sell. Pete was under no illusions that he would be offered next to nothing and he didn't want his mum to get upset over this.

On Friday, he had arranged for two estate agents to value the house and, in the afternoon, he planned to take his mother to see a solicitor. Although she was not keen to discuss it, he thought it would be sensible to update her will, and for the solicitor to set up and witness an Enduring Power of Attorney. If, although he seriously hoped not, she became unable to manage her own affairs then Pete would be able to act for her. He was hoping he could make it into an enjoyable couple of days for his mother by taking her out to lunch at some of their favourite places.

As they approached Harrogate from the Leeds Road direction, Mitsy discovered a lump in her throat. Suddenly she was worried that she would not be able to do this. She hadn't realised quite how she would feel about returning to her home town, virtually as a visitor.

Pete looked over at his mother as they passed by the Stray. Although it wasn't Harrogate's only green space it was always attractive with its avenues of trees; beautiful in springtime when the ornamental cherry trees blossomed and equally pretty through the winter months when tiny white lights festooned the same trees around the perimeter and along the pathways.

Passing by the Pump Room, Mitsy smiled to think of the one occasion that she drank the spa water. It tasted horrible!

The building was now a museum, having been built in the 17th century to house the wells from which the spa waters sprung and which all the well-to-do of the time came to drink for their health. She wondered if the taste was as bad then as it was now.

In no time at all they arrived outside her house. She reminded herself that this had been Pete's home too, so he might also be feeling sad.

She loved that the house had been built from local stone and, like many properties in the area, the slate roof was surrounded by castellations. The pale blue paint on the front door was beginning to show signs of weathering but overall, it was still an attractive home. She hoped that the next owners would appreciate it as much as she and Peter had.

Walking up the front path, she noticed how quickly the weeds had taken hold. Now that was something she didn't miss, the constant worry and effort involved in keeping the garden under control. Unlocking the door, she almost tripped over a heap of post just below the letter box. "I think you can check those over later and either inform the senders of your change of address or put them in the bin!" said Pete. "I will contact the Post Office with your new address so that you will get anything important re-directed."

Mitsy sighed to think of all the extra jobs she was giving Pete, although it was a blessing that he was willing to deal with such matters.

Slowly they walked from room to room while Mitsy put anything she wanted to keep in the carrier bag Pete had thoughtfully brought with him. In fact, there was scarcely anything beyond a few ornaments and the post to take away with her.

A quick glance at the back garden told its own story. Brambles wound themselves through the fence and across what had been a tidy lawn. Opening the back door, she spotted the rose bush that Peter had bought for her one

Valentine's day, flowering vigorously in spite of the overgrowth elsewhere. That reminder of her late husband and all the happy times they had spent here was the trigger for a flood of tears that she was powerless to control. Pete hugged her close until her sobs ceased, "I think we could pick ourselves a lovely bunch of red roses to go in your room at Appledore House, don't you?"

"Yes," said Mitsy, blowing her nose noisily, "especially now I've found my favourite vase."

Having assured himself there was nothing else to take with them, he guided his mother back to the car and then returned to lock up. "Mum. Shall I keep the keys now?" She nodded, still feeling rather distressed.

Driving back, they passed by Valley Gardens and Mitsy recalled the hundreds of times she had taken her sandwiches there to eat during her lunchbreak from her job at the pharmacy. "I do miss Valley Gardens," she told Pete, "but I'm already finding one or two little walks I can do from Appledore House."

Pete knew that she would feel homesick today and he wasn't really sure how to comfort her. "What would you like to do for lunch today? We could go to any of your favourite Harrogate cafés."

"I have an idea actually Pete. We could go to the Standsfield Arms which is just around the corner from Appledore House. I went there last week and the staff are friendly and the lunches are good."

This sounded like evidence that Mitsy was starting to settle in to her new surroundings. Pete was relieved that his mother was beginning to try different things so he was happy to go to the pub as she suggested, on the proviso that he would have to have a non-alcoholic drink as he was driving later.

Lunch did, indeed, turn out pleasantly and the staff recognised her from her first visit. She introduced her son to them and both chose the ploughman's lunch again. It was quite a brief lunch as Pete had to get back to Harrogate to meet the furniture clearance man.

Afterwards, he didn't say much to Mitsy about that encounter, but to be honest he was just relieved that someone would empty the house. He discovered subsequently that several charities were happy to do house clearances for a small fee but he concluded he had probably made the best arrangement because his man was willing to wait until the house was sold and had agreed to take everything, whereas some charities were known to refuse certain items of furniture that they could not recycle, which would still have left him with a problem.

That evening, relaxing in his Travelodge hotel room, he was able to catch up with a few emails for work. Over a drink in the bar, he gave some thought to how he would deal with the estate agents the next morning and, more importantly, how he would encourage his mother to sort out her will.

He needn't have worried, Mitsy had already decided that all her jewellery would go to her nieces (Sky's children) and everything else to Pete. She wished he had a partner, although he seemed to have plenty of friends in Dublin as well as Brussels and all the other places he worked. The last time she asked him if he fancied 'settling down' he laughed and laughed and then explained that he was happier living alone than with the wrong person, which of course made sense. She hadn't raised the subject since.

That night, Mitsy had her usual difficulty going to sleep. Around midnight she woke up with a start, then remembered where she was. After an hour of tossing and turning, she got up. It wasn't cold but she put her dressing gown on anyway. 'I'm not getting up properly, I'll just look out of the window for a few minutes then try to get back to sleep,' she said to herself.

The back garden looked lovely in the light of a full moon. She could see the outline of the larger bushes and the distinctive shape of the monkey puzzle tree. Mr P did keep the garden looking good and it would be a pleasant place to relax when the weather was warm enough.

'Maybe I'll get one of those bird-feeding tables to put outside the window,' she thought. It was something she missed from her old home, the chance to watch the birds throughout the year.

Wandering over to the other side of her room, she noticed how bright everything was, given that the moon amplified the street lights. Nothing was moving anywhere and the whole road was empty. She was just about to turn away to go back to bed when she noticed something strange. Across the road was an old, disused cotton mill. Normally, she gave the building little attention, but she was puzzled to see a distant glow of lights in all the windows. In fact, she thought she could see faint movement through the dusty window panes. 'Well I must be mistaken,' she thought. 'It's probably sleep deprivation!' Misty wasn't one to exaggerate usually, but she couldn't think of any other explanation.

Back in bed she pulled the duvet up round her shoulders and within seconds she fell into a deep and restful sleep.

6

At breakfast Mitsy was tempted to mention her night time observations at the old mill but then it occurred to her that, along with her sighting of the White Lady, people might think she was a bit strange. She decided to keep quiet but check the place over from time to time.

Her friends were concerned as to how she had coped with seeing her former home for the last time, so she was able to reassure them that, although she felt sad, she had valued the chance to collect a few personal items along with the post. She mentioned to the assembled breakfast group that she had brought back some beautifully scented deep red roses from her garden which inevitably led to a couple of people knocking her door later to admire them.

Pete meanwhile had been busy. Happily, the two appointments the next morning were completed highly efficiently and the estate agents had given him their valuations, so he was able to get back to Appledore House well before lunchtime. "Would you like to have lunch here, Pete? I'm sure the kitchen could squeeze an extra portion for you if I asked them now. You could then say hello to some of the other residents; I know they're curious to meet my lovely son!"

Frankly, it was the last thing Pete wanted to do – to eat an institutional meal with a load of grumpy old ladies. To be fair, Appledore House wasn't really like that. One of the reasons he chose it for his mother was that the residents all appeared happy from what he could see in the pictures in the brochure. What really clinched it, was that on his first visit he realised that the place didn't smell stale like some of the other homes that he had visited. It also seemed friendly with a mix of men and women residents. Anyway, it was easiest to say yes to lunch and Mitsy duly went down to the kitchen to see if it would be possible.

I'm not sure what he had expected, but the lightly poached salmon, buttered new potatoes and mixed green vegetables were excellent. Today's cook had introduced a little samphire in with the greens and some of the older folk were quite intrigued as to what it was. Mitsy was quite used to tasting some unusual things as she had got in the habit of eating out regularly when she lived in Harrogate. In any case, she knew from her visits to the fish counter at Sainsbury's that it was samphire.

All in all, lunch was a success and the Appledore residents appreciated the chance to meet Mitsy's son. After the meal, the pair went back to Mitsy's room and Pete broached the subject of updating the will. Mitsy was no fool and she knew this had to be addressed sooner rather than later. The discussion turned out to be painless and the contents of the will were quickly agreed.

In fact, the drive over to Harrogate was in delightful sunshine and Mrs Reed, the solicitor, was so helpful. She took notes of everything Mitsy asked for and promised to send her a draft of the new will in the post as soon as possible, for her agreement. Almost as if Pete had planned it, Mrs Reed asked if she should include an Enduring Power of Attorney 'as most people do these nowadays'. They decided that the signing and witnessing of the new will could be carried out whenever Mitsy could arrange transport. She was fairly sure that Mr Podsiadlo, as the owner of Appledore House, would act as a witness to her will and would even drive her over to the solicitors to conclude the business.

As they drove back, she told Pete about Norma, her new neighbour and a little bit about how she had spent her time this week. Appledore House was well-located and Mitsy was happy to be able to take short walks on level ground directly from the front door. Turning left took her to the corner shop which was also a post office and newsagents. Everyone who served there seemed very pleasant and already they were beginning to recognise her. Turning right about ten minutes' walk away was the pub they had visited, and after quite a distance further, there was a small parade of shops. These included a fish and chip shop, the hairdressers', a chiropodist and an insurance company. She didn't think she was likely to use the latter but she planned to book an appointment with the chiropodist.

Directly opposite the Care Home was the old mill building where Mitsy had seen lights during the night. It had been disused for many years but, according to Jo – one of the care staff – it had been bought by a developer and was to be turned into apartments. She was still puzzling as to whether there were squatters or drug dealers there of an evening so she wisely didn't mention any of that to Pete. He had enough to worry about, she was sure.

Giving his mum a hug before he set off from Appledore House, Pete breathed a sigh of relief that he had managed to fit in everything without causing his mother too much distress and, equally important, he still had ample time to return the hire car and catch his flight back to Dublin. Mitsy returned to room six, feeling tired but happy that they had done everything as planned.

She still felt very sad about Puss the Third and the old house in Harrogate just didn't feel the same without her. When Pete was just a toddler, they went to the Cat's Protection League shelter in York and chose a beautiful tabby cat. Pete insisted on naming her Puss. That child doesn't have a creative bone in his body, she complained to husband Peter when he was next home. To be fair, neither did his father. Puss lived very happily with the Howard family for many years; she gave a good impression of a big, fat fluffy cushion for most of her life.

Before Pete went off to University, Puss died and Mitsy decided it would be good to get another cat for company. Puss the Second was a different character altogether and a skilled mouser. Mitsy hated having to deal with beheaded 'gifts' and worse, but over the years she became inured to this task. Puss the Second was ginger and very clever at pouncing out from behind furniture and throwing her paws around Mitsy's legs in ambush. They definitely had a love/hate relationship. Puss the Second became less nimble as she got older and one day she was knocked down by a car. Mitsy was reluctant to get another cat but Pete pre-empted this decision by arriving home one day with Puss the Third. Puss the Third was a tiny black kitten and Mitsy loved her from the first moment she saw her. She was intelligent and independent and soon learned Mitsy's ways and became the perfect feline companion.

Once Pete had mooted the idea of his mother moving to a care home, Mitsy kept presenting the counter argument that she wouldn't be able to take Puss the Third with her. Various options were reviewed but none of them seemed acceptable or viable. Mitsy was adamant that a cat cannot just be given away 'like a spare television' as she put it. Puss the Third was a living, breathing and fully functioning member of the household and as such deserved proper consideration for her future. In the end, Puss the Third provided her own, dreadfully sad, solution. She quite suddenly developed kidney failure, stopped eating and in a matter of days had to be taken to the vets for her final sleep. Mitsy always felt that Puss the Third knew what was being planned. She missed her gentle presence daily, even though there was a cat that lived nearby and regularly visited the Appledore House garden, it wasn't the same.

She had just decided that she would watch a little light-hearted nonsense on the TV before bed when there was a tap at the door. It was Joyce who was on duty that evening and calling at every resident's room with their medication.

Joyce had worked at Appledore House for several years, arriving from her native Philippine island of Cebu to stay with her elder sister in the north of England. She already had good nursing qualifications and was snapped up by the care home where she had worked ever since. During a brief conversation a few days ago, she discovered that Mitsy had considerable experience of pharmacology from her time working in a pharmacy. Although not professionally qualified, Mitsy had learned a lot over time from the pharmacist himself and had enjoyed that side of the business. Obviously, Joyce had a number of people to see this evening so there wasn't time to talk but as ever she was pleasant, business-like and very careful to ensure that there was nothing that Mitsy needed.

7

Waking early the next morning, Mitsy realised that it was the day for the home's monthly outing. These were organised regularly and residents were invited to take part in what was usually a couple of hours in a minibus, visiting somewhere relatively close by. Mitsy had already been on two trips; the first was to Salts Mill in Saltaire and the second was to the Brontë House in Haworth.

The former textile mill at Saltaire had been converted into an art gallery and a shopping centre with cafés and restaurants. It had many paintings by the local – but now internationally acclaimed - artist David Hockney, some of which were for sale. Mitsy loved the bright colours used by Hockney and would have loved to own one of his swimming pool paintings. Of course, these are valuable and were out of the question for her to buy, so she satisfied herself with some postcard reproductions of his work. The next visit was to the Brontë House and Museum, which was in fact the Parsonage where Charlotte, Emily and Anne Brontë lived and wrote their books. Their brother Branwell lived there too. Again, Mitsy's lively imagination brought the visit to life.

Today's outing for the Appledore residents was to Betty's Tearooms in Harrogate. Given that she had just been to Harrogate twice this week with Pete, it hardly seemed necessary. None-the-less she had already signed up for the trip so she decided that it would do no harm.

After breakfast, Mitsy and Norma found that they were both leaving their rooms at the same time and fell into step, standing together by the front door in readiness for the outing. Norma was well wrapped up in a winter coat, hat, scarf and gloves. She was finding the change in temperature from her South African home quite difficult to adjust to and was already contemplating buying some extra woollen jumpers to aid her transition to the Yorkshire climate. The minibus arrived, parked in the road outside and the pair were thus able to take the two front seats next to the driver and had time to chat, while the other residents arrived in dribs and drabs.

"Mitsy," said Norma, "you know you said that your parents were travellers? Well, did you live in a horse-drawn gypsy caravan?"

"Oh, good grief no!!" replied her neighbour, laughing audibly. "We had an old white van which had a mattress and bunks in the back. It was painted on the outside with the sun, the moon and a rainbow – from what I saw in a couple of photographs, as I don't really remember it."

Norma smiled at her mistake, as she had imagined something much more picturesque.

"We were not Romany or gypsies as such. During the war, mum worked in the cigarette factory and dad was in the RAF. At the time, they lived in 'digs' which they rented. Dad never told us what he did and just used to say it was 'hush-hush' which was a term used in those days for having signed the official secrets act, I believe. After the war, it was difficult to get anywhere to live although they were on a list for a council house and neither of them wanted to live in a pre-fab. As mum and dad liked to tour round folk festivals and poetry happenings, a caravan seemed the answer. Dad was always ready to get out his guitar and accompany himself with his rich, deep voice. He was often invited to play his own compositions although I don't think he got paid much for it in the early days. Once we children grew up, it was not really a suitable way for us to live as we needed to go to school, although I suspect they would have liked to carry on in their rather bohemian lifestyle."

Misty paused for breath, having rarely shared this much information with someone who was almost a stranger. Norma nodded and smiled.

"I suppose it was hard for all of you to adjust to a more settled way of life?" asked Norma, thoughtfully.

"I don't think it made much difference to us kids but it certainly was a complete change for our parents. What happened was that someone up from London heard Dad playing and asked around what people thought of his music. Dad was popular and he received positive reports. The man asked Dad if he would like to write some music for the opening credits of a new radio programme. Dad did that, it went down well and he was asked to do some more. He didn't get paid much but he became recognised as the go-to composer for incidental music. Not long after, he was invited to go to London to discuss some music for a film. Dad quite liked the idea but he wasn't really equipped to do that sort of work from the back of our van. Anyway, they gave him the contract and enough money upfront for him to put down a small deposit on a house. I know you're going to ask me what was the film but I really cannot remember."

Norma nodded again with interest. "What an amazing start to life you had! Mine was very different but challenging in its own way. I was born in the USA then we moved to South Africa for my Dad's work while I was still tiny. I didn't really understand the political situation or apartheid and we lived a comfortable life for a few years, until the demonstrations got too violent and we moved back to the States. That was the pattern for most of my growing up years, moving back and forth, and to be honest, I didn't really know which country was my home. As you can guess, eventually South Africa 'won' when I met and married my husband."

As the minibus started up with a lurch, their conversation stopped. Ruth, one of the care staff, was accompanying them and acting as an unofficial tour guide.

"Ladies and gentlemen, today's outing is taking us to Betty's Tea Room in Harrogate. I will not be giving a running commentary but I'm happy to answer your questions and to point out anything of special interest on the way." As the minibus made its way on a circuitous route skirting the Yorkshire Moors, Mitsy and Norma continued to exchange information about their early years.

As soon as they approached Harrogate, Mitsy noticed that she was feeling much more comfortable than she expected, as well as a sense of pride in her former home town.

In no time at all the minibus was parked near Betty's Tea Room and they all spilled out onto the road in an unruly crowd. Ruth, still acting as unofficial tour guide hurriedly directed everyone to the pavement and went ahead to confirm the booking for their morning stop. As they waited for their teas, coffees and cakes to arrive, Mitsy confided a few more things to Norma.

"You see just down Parliament Street? That was where I used to work. It's not a pharmacy anymore, it's a gift shop now."

"And are we anywhere near your house, Mitsy?"

"Oh no. That's - I mean that it WAS - a large house but not here in the expensive part of town! Actually, it was my parent's house. You know I said that my Dad wrote music for films and things? When I was growing up, he had a studio for his work and we children used to run around in the woods on the edge of town. Over the years the area got built up but we've not driven anywhere near there this morning. Well, Dad was always worried that he was 'selling out to crass commercialisation', as he described it, so eventually when he and Mum were in their sixties, they chose to go back on the road. They bought a very comfortable motorhome and they decided to tour around Europe, meeting up with other musicians and generally exploring new places. They asked Peter and I to look after the house for them. By that stage Rock was no longer with us and Sky was happily settled with her family, so they signed over the house to us. It was very kind, it really helped us a lot."

Mitsy paused as everyone shuffled indoors. Once settled inside the attractive tea rooms, the conversation turned to somewhat more prosaic considerations as everyone chose from the menu and their orders were taken. Raymond had asked if he could join their table and when he went off to look for the gent's toilet Norma, keen to understand her new friend's history, took advantage of his absence to find out a little more.

"What happened when your parents came back from their travels?"

"Oh, they didn't come back to the UK. They settled in France where they both died within six weeks of each other. I believe they were truly happy there."

The friendly waitress at Betty's smiled at these two older folk reminiscing as she placed the food and drinks on the table. The Appledore guests were all enjoying the change of scenery and in fact there was quite a buzz of conversation.

Raymond returned to find his pot of tea and luxury sandwiches were already on the table.

"We didn't wait for you, Raymond, as our cheese rarebit would have got cold!"

"Of course," said Raymond, "there was such a queue I almost gave up!"

Ever the gentleman, he always showed an interest in other people, so much so that few of the other residents knew much about Raymond himself.

"Did I hear you say that you used to work near here, Mitsy?"

Mitsy smiled at the memories. "Yes, Raymond. It was a pharmacy at the bottom of Parliament Street. It was a lovely shop with perfumes, after-shave, cosmetics, lots of pretty things for hair and nails etc and of course, the pharmaceuticals. We sold lots of over-the-counter medicines as well as distributing prescription drugs. It's funny how these days there are adverts regularly on the TV telling people to ask the pharmacist for advice instead of waiting to see a GP. That used to be the norm back then. I always enjoyed helping people in that way and often we had something useful on the shelves that would sort the problem out."

"That is very much the approach we have in Port Elizabeth. Of course, we have good healthcare services in general with both state-run and private hospitals."

Norma rarely spoke about her home city and as Mitsy sensed that she was still really homesick, she didn't ask too many questions. However, she did notice that Norma tended to speak about Port Elizabeth in the present tense and she realised that in time she would need to accept that this move was permanent.

"I've never been to South Africa. Have you, Raymond?"

"Actually, I have," he responded, much to the surprise of the two women.

"When my wife and I retired, we went on a magnificent cruise that gave us the opportunity to visit KwaZulu Natal, the Drakensberg mountains, Johannesburg and the vineyards of Cape Town. It was a marvellous experience and I'm only sorry we didn't get to the 'Windy City' which I believe your home town is called, Norma."

Norma beamed with delight and the conversation continued, ranging over Raymond's observations and Norma's happy recollections. Well, I never, thought Mitsy to herself. How pleasant it is for these two to discuss their past and both clearly are enjoying it. At least they are not directing their questions at me, not that I mind, but it's good to be a listener too.

Before long, Ruth quietly called round each table where her charges were sitting, to make sure all was well and to tell them they had another ten minutes before they would need to pay their bills and head for the coach. This prompted a flurry of walking sticks as everyone headed at the same time for the toilets. Ruth, being an old hand at these things was expecting a considerable delay and had allowed for a twenty-minute hiatus.

Ruth had come to the care profession later in her life, having been a primary school teacher for many years. Frankly, there was not a lot of difference between handling a class of seven-year olds on an outing and this group, although she would never dream of telling them so!

Many of the staff at Appledore had been there for several years and Mitsy had met all of them during her first few weeks. The home was privately owned by Mr and Mrs Podsiadlo. Most people called her Mrs P although a few staff risked calling her Hannah when there was no one else around. Hannah's husband, a Polish airman, was a member of the Allied Forces during the second world war and the couple came to the UK after their home town near Poznan was occupied by German troops. Hannah was well liked by staff and residents alike. Over time, she had employed a senior nurse to take over some of her duties and Greg, the 'odd-job' man was promoted to head of maintenance. Everyone thought that was quite funny because Greg had no staff and continued to do all the odd jobs he had always done.

Having shepherded everyone back on to the minibus, Ruth felt she could relax, trusting that not much could go wrong in the next hour on the drive back to Appledore House, as was the case.

Both Norma and Mitsy were quiet on the return journey. It had been an enjoyable trip even if it had been tiring. The passing scenery was pleasant and virtually everyone was silent with their own thoughts, or nodding off in the warmth of the vehicle.

Arriving home, Mitsy was approached immediately by Mrs P who said she had some good news for her. It transpired that Mitsy's sister Sky was planning to visit and had phoned the Home to find out when would be a good time. This was not 'good news' and Mitsy was not pleased about it. For one thing, Sky could have phoned back when she was in, rather than making an arrangement behind her back as if she wasn't capable of such decision making herself. Secondly, she and Sky didn't really get on and she wasn't sure she could face several hours of Sky moaning about her husband and daughters. None-the-less, she said nothing to Mrs P as it really was a personal matter. It had been decided that Sky would visit next Tuesday for lunch, travelling by train and leaving late afternoon.

Although it really wasn't necessary, Mitsy began tidying her room, as if Sky would notice anyway. It was her way of getting her thoughts in order and she was trying hard to dispel her grumpy mood.

Try and look at it from Sky's point of view, she said to herself. She is no doubt a bit concerned that you require looking after in a care home. Rubbish, she replied. Sky doesn't care about anyone apart from herself. On the other hand, how awful can it be to listen to Sky's complaints about her lovely husband and two children, who of course are grown up and have their own lives to lead now, despite their mother's interference? The visit will soon be over and life can return to its calm and gentle pace.

In spite of speaking severely to herself and reflecting on the kindness of her own son Pete, she still felt irritated that her sister could disturb her so. Sky wasn't even here yet and she was being a nuisance!

As she paced around her room feeling annoyed, the dinner bell rang. Much as she wanted to phone her sister and question the visiting arrangements, she resisted the urge knowing that she would regret her ill-tempered reaction afterwards, so she headed off to the dining room, quietly fuming. Family! They drive you mad sometimes. Mitsy began to relax once the meal was served. It was fish fingers, creamy mashed potato, baby carrots and broccoli spears drizzled with butter. Whilst it wasn't gourmet fare, it was hot, tasty, and easy for her to eat with her clumsy and recalcitrant hands. The day she moved in, the staff had very kindly found some lightweight cutlery which she could handle and at every meal these were laid out for her without a mention of her difficulties. She knew she was very fortunate to have such kind people around her. However, she couldn't help - just once in a while – thinking of the superb meals she used to eat in the Harrogate restaurants with Peter. She so enjoyed all kinds of delicious seafood, such as lobster, or the locally raised beef or lamb. Even after Peter had passed away, she sometimes treated herself to a meal out in town with friends.

There was a gentle hum of conversation at the meal table, which got a little louder once the plates were cleared away and everyone waited expectantly for dessert. There were two cooks on duty at all times and today's pair were Julie and Sam. Sam had not long left school and was working towards his National Vocational Qualifications so he was always very pleased if someone praised his cooking. After the meal, he could write down the feedback in his NVQ portfolio, along with a picture of his offering. Today it was rhubarb crumble and custard, which elicited murmurs of enjoyment from around the table. It was such a pleasure to see his happy face, even though Mitsy would have preferred ice cream, finding that custard always brought back unwelcome memories of school dinners.

8

It had actually been a restful weekend and Mitsy had almost forgotten that Sky was due to visit her on Tuesday. After having spent a couple of days with Pete, she realised that sorting out the old house had been quite a relief. The red roses they brought back from her old garden still gave off a heady perfume and she could imagine that Peter was there with her. She thought that her late husband would have been happy to see her settled in this comfortable room in Appledore House, making friends and taking part in group activities. She had always been rather solitary and enjoyed her own company but since moving in she had found that someone else to talk to was pleasant occasionally.

This morning a woman was coming to run a craft group. Mitsy was uncertain whether to take part, or whether to continue her internet search. The latter had taken a back seat recently and she felt she ought to get on with it. The trouble was, it always seemed more like work, rather than pleasure.

Norma knocked on Mitsy's door. "Are you coming to the craft group? I didn't really want to go on my own," she said. Mitsy smiled, "Well I was in two minds but I'll be happy to come. Just let me get my specs and handbag." She didn't confide her trepidations that whatever it was they were going to be asked to make would be too difficult for her arthritic hands but instead headed off down the corridor towards the main lounge or sitting area with Norma hurrying behind her.

Lucy was already there, also Arthur. They were chatting quietly until Mitsy and Norma arrived. "We were just saying how surprised we were to find so many foreigners here," said Lucy, directing her gaze towards Mitsy. Initially, Mitsy was entirely puzzled by her comment.

"I'm afraid I don't really know what you mean?" she replied.

"Oh, you know. Most of the nurses are black and also the care assistants."

"To be honest, I don't notice the colour of people's skin," she responded. "I find it interesting to know what countries some people have come from and to think about how difficult it must have been to learn another language, adjust to the climate, the food and even gain additional qualifications here. I'm full of admiration for them. I imagine that many of the staff here are second generation in any case." Mitsy hoped that this conversation would end as she certainly didn't like the direction it was heading in.

Fortunately, the person who would be running the craftwork session came in the door at this moment. As luck would have it, or perhaps not, she appeared to be a woman of colour too.

"Hello, I'm Jeannie. I'm Joyce's sister. I'm here to run the craft group today. Does anyone know how many people we are expecting?"

Arthur leapt up, rising to his not inconsiderable height, to look at the list pinned on the noticeboard. "There will be about ten," he said.

"Right, we'll wait until everyone is here."

Mitsy really hoped that Jeannie did not hear the conversation that had been taking place as she arrived, so she said: "It's good to meet you Jeannie! I presume your birthplace was also Cebu, like Joyce? It must be a beautiful island."

Jeannie smiled with the warmth of the welcome and nodded. The remainder of the group appeared suddenly at the door and everyone settled down to find out what Jeannie had planned for them. It involved making greeting cards for

Christmas, Easter and birthdays. They were all given card, scissors, a pot of glue and pretty things to stick on them. There were also silver and gold lettered greetings for every type of card one could think of. Mitsy sighed as she knew she would not be able to cut out anything.

"I think it might be a good idea for you to work in pairs," suggested Jeannie.

Norma moved to be nearer to Mitsy, "I'll cut, if you do the sticking," she said, thoughtfully. They worked quietly for some forty minutes, showing their creations to 'the teacher' as they jokingly referred to Jeannie. When the class came to an end, they were told they could keep any finished cards. Jeannie packed up quickly and left, after everyone thanked her for an interesting and enjoyable session.

Mitsy felt she had left some things unsaid from the conversation at the beginning of the morning, but decided not to stir things up – yet! She had little patience with narrow or bigoted views, even though she knew these could often stem from ignorance and lack of education or limited life experiences.

Later that afternoon, Mitsy decided to take a short walk. On leaving Appledore House, she turned left and headed for the corner shop. She needed to buy some shampoo although that wasn't the real reason for her walk. She wanted to have a closer look at the old mill and she intended to make it appear as if she just casually happened to be on the other side of the road.

At the corner shop she picked up a copy of the Telegraph & Argus, the local paper, and her favourite shampoo. Strolling back, she crossed over the road and ambled down the pavement on the far side, on her way back to Appledore House.

Ahead, she could see the mill. No one would say it was beautiful but it was the classic textile mill architecture from the time it was built. It was four storeys high and constructed from mellowed local stone. The slate roof was probably the only part that was in relatively good condition. The rather plain, Georgian style windows with small panes and sash cord fittings were thick with dirt and dust although the main entrance had a very grand portico and looked as if, in its heyday, this doorway was set aside for the mill owner and his wealthy gentlemen friends. The building was in such a bad state that some of the ground floor windows had been boarded up and the big mill chimney even had a tree growing out of the top.

There was a large For Sale sign at the right-hand end of the building, which she wouldn't have been able to see from her window. All in all, she concluded that no one was living or even squatting there. It was the epitome of derelict.

Crossing back across the road to her home, Mitsy noticed for the first time that the wisteria that grew across the front of Appledore House was beginning to blossom. In the past, Appledore must have been a really stylish property, she thought.

Back in room six, she kicked off her shoes, and sat down to peruse the local paper. There was not much to interest her and once she had hastily flicked past the obituaries and the job adverts, she was on the point of folding it up and putting it in the bin when she spotted a very small news item:

Planning permission declined for old cotton mill. Developers have been turned down for the third time in their bid to convert the historic mill into twenty-three luxury apartments. Planners stated environmental concerns from increased traffic and inadequate parking for the proposed new homes as the main reason for the refusal.

Mitsy could see clearly from the picture that it was the mill opposite Appledore House. Thus, she was satisfied that her outing today had been worthwhile.

A knock at the door revealed Jo, bringing afternoon tea and biscuits. Mitsy thanked her and asked if she didn't ever have time off. "Oh, I certainly do Mitsy; it's just that Maggie is not well so I'm covering for her for a couple of days. It's only a cold but Mrs Podsiadlo prefers us not to work if we have anything that the residents could catch."

Turning to her laptop, Mitsy logged on and began to get underway with tracing her mother's family tree. Strangely enough, she had had very little to do with that side of the family, probably because her grandparents had remained in Ireland and couldn't afford to visit very often. I do wish I'd asked Mum more about our family history before she died, she thought. It wasn't that there were any secrets, probably, but it just wasn't a topic of conversation.

After more than an hour of searching, she had identified the name of her great grandmother and ascertained that she had been a seamstress. That was amusing because neither Mitsy herself nor her own mother had any interest or natural ability in sewing or making things with their hands. She concluded that that particular family trait had died out back in Ireland.

She was unable to track down her grandfather at all, which was frustrating. It occurred to her that she might ask Sky tomorrow to see if she remembered anything about him. Having reached what seemed like a brick wall, Mitsy decided that was enough for today. She already had 'screen eyes' and didn't want to look too tired for Sky's visit in the morning.

Norma had asked Mitsy to call round when she felt like it, so this was a good opportunity to do so. Norma was delighted to have a visit from her neighbour and Mitsy was fascinated to see how Norma's room differed from hers. It was considerably smaller but already Norma had made it homely with her pictures from South Africa and personal ornaments. They chatted for half an hour which was just enough for them both.

Relaxing in bed later, Mitsy reflected on the day and realised she had been rather busy. She had intended for it to be restful, so she could mentally prepare herself for Sky's visit but in spite of all that had happened she did not feel her usual foreboding before seeing her sister and for the first time in many days she slept well all night.

9

Sky arrived just before eleven o'clock. Mrs P was looking out of her bedroom window and saw her approaching Appledore House. She hurried down the grand staircase and was ready to open the door to welcome Mitsy's guest, before escorting her along the corridor to room six. Mrs P noticed, quite perceptively, that the two sisters did not hug or kiss.

Sky's appearance did not really live up to her colourful and exotic name. She was wearing a sensible, brown pleated skirt which fell to below her knees and a hand-knitted pullover in dark green, both of which were covered by a voluminous grey checked winter coat. Her wavy, auburn hair had long ago turned grey but this was barely visible. On some women, wearing a navy beret can look totally chic but on Sky, who insisted on pulling it down over her ears, she was somewhat reminiscent of the comedian Benny Hill. Her dark brown, flat lace-up shoes completed the ensemble. No one would have dreamed that these two were sisters.

Mitsy was, in fact, pleased to see Sky in her own way. She showed her round her room, pointing out the garden view and the well-appointed en suite bathroom.

"Do sit down, Sky, you must be tired after your long journey," she said with her customary kindness, ushering her sibling to the nearest armchair. This was all the invitation Sky needed to launch into her diatribe about the state of public transport, the difficulty of getting to Mitsy's new home which was 'in the back of beyond' before offering an appraisal of Appledore House.

"I don't know why you wanted to give up our family home in Harrogate. You had everything you wanted there and this – this place – is no more than a bedsit."

Before Sky could rant on any more, Mitsy interrupted to put her side of the argument: "Now you know very well why I had to move, Sky. Our old house was much too big for me to look after, given that my arthritis has got worse over the years which made everything difficult. Appledore House is lovely; it's like being in a friendly hotel with all my washing, cleaning, cooking done for me. If, later on, I'm less able to look after myself I shall be in the best place because Pete cannot keep coming over from Dublin to do things. I'm happy here."

She actually thought that it was more like a luxury hotel but she didn't want Sky to think she had that much money to spare. It hadn't really been an issue between them that their parents gave the house to her and Peter and in any case, they still had to pay the outstanding mortgage over the remaining years.

That stopped Sky for a short while, so that she could draw breath and give an update on all the supposedly dreadful things Jim, her husband, had done. Mitsy found this was one of the most distressing aspects about seeing her sister because in truth, Jim was a sweetheart who would do anything for his wife. Somehow, Sky just liked to moan about everyone and anything.

She was just gearing up for a grumble about her two daughters when the bell rang to let people know a meal was being served. Sky was in the process of suggesting this was all too regimented, commenting that 'it's like being in prison' but Mitsy just raised her voice over hers: "Ah. Lovely! Food is ready. Do you need to use the bathroom? I do hope you will join us for lunch?" and without waiting for an answer she steered her sister down the corridor to the dining room.

47

The other residents were all very friendly towards Sky and extremely sympathetic about the journey she had endured in order to visit Mitsy. Of course, it wasn't anything like as bad as Sky was making out but they weren't to know that this was Sky's habitual demeanour. Mitsy was thankful that nothing too contentious came up in discussion over the dinner table. It was also an absolute blessing that the chicken casserole with new potatoes and runner beans was delicious. Sky enjoyed her meal and was very complimentary about the lemon meringue pie for afters. Sam beamed with pleasure, as it was the first time he'd attempted this dessert.

Back in room six, Mitsy asked tentatively when Sky needed to catch her train and whether she would like to have a taxi booked to take her to the station. It transpired that Sky had already booked the same taxi she had used for her outward journey and that she had less than half an hour to wait for his arrival.

"Right. That's good. Well, there's just time to ask you, what you can remember of Grandad O'Neill? I'm doing an internet search on our family and anything you can remember would be useful."

Sky did not use the internet, neither did she have a mobile phone, so Mitsy's easy facility with IT really annoyed her. On the other hand, she liked being asked her opinion so she wracked her brains to think of any useful information.

"I think grandad used to smoke a pipe," she began. Mitsy tried hard not to sigh audibly, given that this gem was hardly going to elucidate her search of the births and deaths registers. "Oh, and he played the, what was it called?"

There was a long pause and Mitsy was about to offer a list of instruments as options when there was a tap on the door. "Your taxi has arrived," said Ruth.

Sky seemed happy to be departing and as she pulled on her coat it was as if she had all but forgotten anything to do with their grandfather.

Mitsy accompanied her sister to the door, ushering her into the taxi and wishing her a safe journey home. "Give me a call when you get in, please."

Thus it was that when the phone rang much later that evening, for an instant Mitsy wondered who could be calling at this time of night.

"It's me. Terrible journey. I've only just got home. By the way, it's penny whistle." She hung up, leaving Mitsy shaking her head with disbelief.

Remarkably, Mitsy slept well. Perhaps it was relief that Sky's visit was over or maybe she was just exhausted and her body took control of her circadian rhythms and insisted she got some rest. There could have been another reason. She had agreed to another lunchtime get-together with Arthur, who was turning into a kind and thoughtful friend.

10

"Thank you, Arthur. I believe it's my turn to get lunch today."

"Certainly not, dear lady. I insist on being an old-fashioned and hopefully well-mannered gentleman. This was my invitation and I enjoy your company. Now, do tell me what your news is!"

Mitsy had been looking forward to telling Arthur what she had recently discovered. Having drawn a blank for the time being on her grandfather's background via her ancestry search and having failed to extract any useful information from her sister Sky, she had decided to look into the history of the old mill opposite. Her shopping expedition had uncovered that the property was due to be sold and converted by a property developer. Of course, it could be months or years before anything was done to the derelict building, given that planning permission had been turned down.

"Well. I think I already told you that the old mill opposite us here at Appledore House is for sale. I thought it would be interesting to know a bit of its history before it is turned into luxury apartments."

Arthur nodded silently as he tucked into his ploughman's lunch.

"It used to be called Park Mill and I think it was built in 1870. It was a steam powered textile mill and it was a very busy place for many years. There's nothing really romantic about it; for the employees it was hard, dirty work and probably only marginally better than being in the workhouse. I'm just going to eat some of this delicious ploughman's lunch and then I'll tell you more. Oh! They've given us pickled onions today. Aren't they big?! I'm not sure I can cut mine."

Mitsy chattered on, quite happy to be out and sharing her news with Arthur. He, meanwhile, leant over carefully and sliced her large pickled onion in half.

"The information about the working conditions was what really shocked me. I suppose I shouldn't be surprised but...."

They sat in companionable silence for a few minutes, taking a sip of their drinks and enjoying the lunch. Peter the pub dog was settled into his usual place stretched out on the large rug in front of the open fire.

"So, people were employed to work a thirteen- to sixteen-hour working day, even the children. The conditions were truly dreadful. Several historians commented on the nasty smelling pollution which apparently was worse in Bradford than many of the other mill towns. This was bad both inside and outside the mill. The air was hot and humid, it was full of cotton dust and the noise was atrocious. Inside, everyone managed to communicate only by lip-reading. No conversation was permitted at all unless it related to work. Many people went completely deaf after a couple of months because there was no ear protection. The workers were responsible for the machinery and if anything went wrong or if any tools were lost, they had to pay for them.

I also discovered that pauper apprentices and orphans were employed from the age of nine years. They were given lodgings, food and one hour of schooling per week. Sadly, there were lots of accidents.

Oh, I could go on Arthur, but you will get the picture. Of course, the mill owner became very wealthy on the back of this abuse. In some ways, I wish I hadn't looked into it."

They both sighed.

"That's very sad Mitsy, but it is how it was back then. Shall I tell you a bit more about the history of Appledore House? It may actually restore your faith in human nature."

Mitsy smiled, because of course she was basically a positive thinker, she was just being honest to Arthur about her emotional reaction to learning about the mill.

"Well, before Appledore House was handed over to the Red Cross in 1916, it was owned by John Doughty. The house had been in the family for several generations and handed down the male line, most of whom were merchants. At the start of the first world war in July 1914, Doughty's only son volunteered for the armed forces and was very quickly sent overseas. Doughty, his wife and daughter remained in the area in the hope that this 'war to end all wars' would be over quickly, if not by Christmas.

When the war seemed likely to continue, the county branch of the British Red Cross sought premises to provide an Auxiliary Hospital for wounded soldiers back from the front. Appledore House seemed ideal and Violet and her mother both joined the Voluntary Aid Detachment. They were trained in first aid and home nursing, reporting first to the matron and then the commandant who was in overall control.

When they received news that John junior had died of his injuries in battle, the family were heartbroken. In some ways, it may have strengthened Violet's resolve to do whatever she could to save other young men from the same fate. She certainly would have heard from the injured soldiers some tales of the horrific conditions in the trenches and must have wondered what exactly had happened to her beloved brother."

Misty's vivid imagination could almost picture how the old house was being used at that time.

"Now, I've got quite a lot more to uncover," said Arthur, "but I have a sneaking suspicion that your ghostly White Lady could be Violet."

"Oh, how lovely! The White Lady was a young woman and she certainly had a kindly and caring expression," said Mitsy.

Lunch over, Mitsy and Arthur strolled back to Appledore House in the sunshine. It was good to have a friend to share things with, thought Mitsy.

11

Although Mitsy thought that she had probably met everyone in the home, there were several residents that she felt she hardly knew. It was interesting therefore, to have someone new knock on her door this morning shortly after breakfast.

"I hope I'm not calling round at an inconvenient time?" asked Caitlin. "We haven't really spoken since you moved in and I hoped we could be friends. My name is Caitlin although everyone calls me Kate."

"Hello Kate. Yes, I've seen you around but haven't yet managed to sit near you for a chat, at mealtimes. Do come in!"

"What a lovely room! Mine is upstairs and although it has pleasant views of the roof tops and the bottom of the garden it is not nearly as spacious."

Mitsy explained how her room seemed larger because it had accommodated a couple of people previously.

"Why don't you tell me a little about yourself and then I'll do the same," suggested Kate.

In this way, by the time Ruth was bringing round the mid-morning coffee these two had got to know each other so much better.

"Fancy us both having links to Dublin," said Kate. "I know it's a big city but it's definitely a small world! I haven't been there for years, so I suppose it has changed."

"I'm hoping to go over to Dublin for a few days, to stay with my son. He has an apartment in the city. Would you like to come too? Pete's got two spare rooms so it wouldn't be any trouble."

Kate looked surprised but very unsure of the generous offer and Mitsy thought perhaps Kate didn't have the money for a flight, or was just wary of travelling. "Think about it. No need to decide now. I intended to go for three days midweek as soon as the weather gets warmer." "Thank you, Mitsy. I will think about it but now I should leave you in peace – we've been chatting almost all the morning!"

This morning's conversation had reassured Mitsy that, even though she had left behind a number of friends in Harrogate, it was still possible to develop new relationships. She was especially encouraged that everyone respected her personal space, by not overstaying their welcome in room six. It was something that had worried her a great deal before she moved in to Appledore House. For most of her married life she had lived quite an independent existence and she was reluctant to give that up now.

When Peter was away at sea, although they were mostly able to communicate by phone or letter, she was responsible for the home, their son and herself. She had built up quite a supportive network of friends who were always ready to help on the rare occasions she needed to ask, and by the same token she was always happy to help them.

Being self-sufficient had its funny side too. Once Pete was at school, she looked for a part-time job, partly for the money and partly for adult conversation. In those early years before Pete got to secondary school then university, she took on all sorts of jobs. These included working as a lunchtime barmaid; waitressing; shop assistant in a dress shop; cleaner; receptionist in a hairdressing salon; school dinner lady and many other roles. Her husband used to joke that he was never sure who he was coming home to. In fact, he once opened the door and called out, "I'm home!! Who are you today my darling?" Eventually, Mitsy settled down to her job in the pharmacy and put an end to the swapping and changing. These varied jobs did, in any case, give her a chance to meet lots of people around the town and there was always something new and interesting to learn.

It occurred to her that as she had offered accommodation in Pete's apartment to her friend, it would be polite to ask Pete if he had any objection. Her quick email got a speedy response:

Hi Pete when you were over here, we talked about me coming to Dublin to stay with you for a couple of days. I'm not planning to visit yet but I just wondered if you would mind if I brought a friend? She has family links to the city and I thought it would be nice to have a companion with me. Hope you are OK? Love Mum xxx

Hi Mum Yes that would be fine, of course. Don't leave it too long! Love Pete xxx

That evening, Mitsy had another one of her sleepless nights. She could not think of anything that was troubling her specifically, but no matter how she tried to relax and drop off, sleep eluded her.

Eventually, she stopped battling with her insomnia and decided she would get up, get dressed and go in search of a warming mug of tea in the kitchen, where she knew someone would be sitting. So often this was the solution, a few minutes chatting to one of the staff and not worrying about her difficulty sleeping, generally calmed her enough to drop off to sleep once she got back to her room.

Glancing through the window as she pulled on some trousers and a pullover, she noticed that some lights were showing in the mill again. It is odd, she thought.

As she walked along the ground floor corridor, she wondered if she would see the White Lady again. She was still calling her this, in her head, although there was now a possibility that she was Violet, as Arthur had suggested. No

White Lady was to be seen, so she headed into the kitchen and was pleased to find Julie on duty and apparently peeling potatoes for tomorrow's meal.

"I am sorry to be a nuisance, Julie, but I couldn't sleep and I wondered if I could have a cup of tea, please?"

Julie was happy to oblige as it could be a long night on duty without company. Sometimes she dozed off, but she was wide awake and only too happy to put the kettle on. She liked Mitsy, much as she did the majority of residents. One or two were a bit trying but mostly they were manageable with a smile and a kind word.

Once the tea was drunk, Mitsy was still feeling alert and restless so she mentioned to Julie the lights that she could see from her room in the old mill.

"Shall I let you into a secret?" said Julie in a conspiratorial manner. "We always sit in the kitchen when we're on night duty because it's warm. There's a room behind here, which leads directly outdoors. Shall we go and have a quick look at the old mill from here?"

And so it was that the room behind the kitchen revealed a side door to Appledore House that only the staff knew about and used. Mitsy was under the impression that it was never locked, which meant they could come and go easily without ringing the front door bell which would disturb the residents at night.

The pair walked very quietly round the side of the building and once they got to the gravelled driveway it was obvious that there were no lights on in the mill. "Oh, maybe I dreamt it. Thank you, Julie, for the tea and for putting my mind at rest."

Mitsy hurried back to her room, determined to go to sleep now. She even resisted the temptation to look out of her own window. I'm a silly woman with an overactive imagination, she said to herself. As she at last drifted off to sleep, she imagined having a conversation with Violet.

12

It was around ten o'clock after Mitsy had enjoyed some breakfast and was back in her room, putting on her coat and getting ready to head off down the road for her appointment with the chiropodist, when she could hear voices in the corridor. Raymond was obviously talking to someone. Mitsy didn't see much of him, even though he was her nearest neighbour because he usually had breakfast in his room. In fact, he would probably have asked for all his meals in his room – being quite a shy man – were it not that Mrs P encouraged him to socialise from time to time.

Mitsy thought she'd wait until the speakers moved away before she went out, then there was a tentative knock on the door.

It was Kate, looking rather sheepish. "Oh, Mitsy I'm sorry to trouble you just as you are going out."

"That's no problem Kate, what can I do for you?"

"May I come in for a moment?"

Mitsy stood to one side and gestured to her new friend to take a seat.

Kate took a deep breath before speaking. "I'm afraid I cannot come to Dublin with you; you see I'm terrified of flying. I've been worrying all night what a fool you will think I am but I just can't do it."

Mitsy smiled sympathetically. "Oh, you mustn't be concerned about that. It was only an off-the-cuff suggestion of mine. Plenty of people are unhappy about flying. I bet some of them pretend they are being 'green' when really they just don't want to fly."

"Thank you for being so understanding, Mitsy. I've only been on a plane once and I hated it. But I wondered if you would check on my family connections for me when you visit your son?"

Mitsy must have looked puzzled, almost as if she was being asked to call on a stranger's grandmother.

"If you could look up some things for me at the Dublin Registrar's Office for Births, Deaths and Marriages, I'd really appreciate it."

"Well, of course I could. But couldn't you check all that yourself on line?"

"Oh dear no. I don't know how to use the internet but I thought you could just pop in for me while you are there?"

The previous day, Mitsy had briefly explained to Kate that one of her hobbies was researching about her ancestors. She had emphasised that it was fun, interesting and all you had to do was make a note of all the known information of family names, birthdays, weddings etc and use that as a basis for building a family tree. It had never occurred to her that Kate couldn't use the internet, although it appeared that she was not alone in this and there were plenty of people at Appledore House who were unfamiliar with the use of the world wide web.

"You see, I've made a note of the limited information I've got for you to use as a starting point," she smiled, hopefully.

"Right. Well, I can make a start for you but I cannot promise to get far. It's a very time-consuming exercise and sometimes one reaches a dead end. I'm sorry Kate but I have an appointment to keep, so I have to go out. I'll put your notes safely in my folder for now and I'll look at them later."

With that she dashed off, not wishing to arrive late for her first appointment with a new chiropodist.

It was only as she walked back, with a lilt in her step now that her feet had been expertly tended to, that she began to reflect on the exchange with Kate early this morning. She could see that she might be getting more than one enquiry from her fellow residents, which would turn what she had seen as a gentle private hobby into a never-ending chore. She concluded that the best thing she could do would be to check on a couple of things for Kate and then say she couldn't find out anything else. She would also need to be alert to other people looking for help. It perhaps wasn't a kind thought but Mitsy did wonder if this was the sole reason that Kate had called round in the first instance, asking to be friends.

Back in room six, she decided to arrange her trip to see Pete as soon as possible. She hadn't actually visited him in Dublin for almost three years and it was an interesting city with lots to offer. Come to think of it, she hadn't actually been away anywhere recently as all her time had been focussed on the move to Appledore House. She decided that she deserved a little treat and it would be a good opportunity to do some clothes shopping too!

> Hi Pete. Just letting you know that it will just be me staying as it turns out that my friend doesn't like flying. Any idea when would be a good time to come over? Love Mum xx

Almost immediately a new email pinged into her inbox:

> Hi Mum. I'd love to see you any time. Next week is quiet, after that I have a string of meetings in Brussels, Helsinki and Stockholm over the next few weeks. See what you can arrange! Love Pete xxx

Mitsy immediately searched the internet for suitable flights and replied:

Pete. I can get an evening flight this Thursday, leaves Leeds/Bradford at 19:25 arrives Dublin 20:30. There's a return flight on Sunday at 20:25 which gets me in 21:55. That should be OK, especially if I can get a lift to the airport from Mr P. Shall I book? Love Mum xxx

Pete's instant response was for his mother to go ahead. When she closed her laptop, she felt quite excited. It was only a short trip but it would be lovely to see some familiar places in Dublin, as well as spending a little time with Pete.

13

Thursday afternoon found Mitsy packing her small overnight bag and checking and rechecking its contents. Mr Podsiadlo had agreed to take Mitsy to the airport and, even more importantly, to collect her late on Sunday evening. I must bring back some Irish whiskey for him, as a thank you, she said to herself.

Fortunately, all went well on the drive to Yeadon, which is where Leeds/Bradford airport is located. Mitsy's flight was on time and the pilot announced that they would probably arrive in well under the hour, as the wind was with them. There was hardly time to settle in her seat, read the safety instructions and drink the coffee that was provided by the friendly stewardess before the descent began. The man sitting next to her seemed impressed that an 'older lady' as he chose to call her, was confidently travelling alone and although he meant well, Mitsy had no intention of telling him her business.

As she was only carrying hand luggage, she was swiftly off the plane and first in the taxi queue. The taxi driver was courteous and given it was barely a twenty-minute drive at this time of night, she was dropped off outside Pete's apartment at Aston Quay shortly after nine o'clock.

Mitsy had only brought with her a few euros, enough to pay for the taxi but she realised she would need to change some more sterling while she was here.

After big hugs and not a little teasing of Pete's efforts to tidy his home before his mother's visit, what was left of the evening was spent in planning how to spend the next couple of days. Pete had to go to work on Friday, so Mitsy explained about Caitlin and her commitment to do a little ancestry search for her. She also was keen to do some clothes shopping for herself so that really wrapped up the whole of the next day.

"I shall cook a meal for you tomorrow evening and I've got some ideas about what we could do on Saturday," said Pete.

"In which case, I shall take you out for dinner that evening," she replied. "We can just laze around on Sunday before my return."

Whether she was feeling relaxed with Pete around, or tired after her journey, Mitsy fell asleep straight away and did not wake up once in the night. By the time she realised it was morning, Pete had gone to work, leaving her a light breakfast on the kitchen table, a spare key and a note saying when he hoped to be home.

Fortunately, the weather was looking fair and Mitsy was thankful she had not had to carry a waterproof or heavy winter coat. She set off around ten o'clock and walked along the quayside, enjoying the fresh air and the unfamiliar sights. Following instructions that Pete had given her, she turned right after City Quay down Lombard Street, easily finding numbers 12 to 14 where the Registry Office was located.

The member of staff on duty (Mitsy didn't know whether to call her the Registrar) helpfully showed her where to find the records that she was looking for. "Hmm. In some ways this is more interesting than doing an internet search," she remarked to the woman. Checking all the information that Kate had given her on the sheet of paper, it took only a short time to find some of the documents requested and she took out her notepad and pen to write down the salient points.

"Would you like a copy of those?" asked the woman. "There is a twenty-euro charge per page."

Mitsy checked her purse and found she had enough to pay for one page, so she selected the registration of the birth that Kate had asked for and made brief notes on the details from the other two.

She was pleased she had managed to get the information Kate had asked her for, but quite puzzled by what she had found. Leaving the registrar's office, she headed back towards the city centre until she came across a suitable coffee shop in which to sit down and relax.

'Well, I never,' she said to herself as she looked at the papers carefully. 'I think I shall have to be careful how to break this news to Kate when I get back to Appledore House.'

After a coffee, a pastry and a little rest in the coffee shop, she decided it was time to do some of the things for herself that she had in mind. Crossing the beautiful river Liffey at O'Connell Bridge, she made her way towards the shops in Grafton Street. By mid-afternoon she was carrying several bags with some special additions to her wardrobe including a new pair of leather boots and some luxury make-up. She had topped up her fund of euros, so she had enough to pay for the meal the next day, taxis and some to spare for another visit. Mitsy was feeling very tired now, so she decided to take a taxi back to Pete's flat.

Mitsy had always loved driving and the freedom it offered but as she got older, she realised that she was using her car less and less frequently and her driving confidence was waning. Eventually, she gave her car to one of her nieces whose need was much greater than hers. Since giving up driving, she tried to make sure that she always had enough money with her to pay for a taxi if it was necessary.

Pete had no need for a car while he lived here in Dublin. His office was a ten-minute walk away and everything else was close by. He had an account with the taxi firm that he used for his regular journeys to and from the airport, which was paid for by his employers.

When Pete got in from work, he sat with his mother for a short while so that she could recount how her day had panned out. She was so excited to show him her shopping purchases he didn't have the heart to remind her that she had to carry these all back to the UK along with her overnight bag.

"Now, Pete. Look at this with me, will you?" she said, digging out the documents relating to her friend Kate. "What do you make of this?"

Pete carefully perused all the evidence and then turned to his mother. "Well, it looks to me as if your friend's sister was actually her mother."

"That's what I thought. There's no father's name and the people who she called Mam and Dad were actually her grandparents."

"Good lord! Doesn't she know?"

"I don't think so, but on the other hand she may have had a suspicion and that may have been why she asked me to look into it. Whatever do I do?"

"Well, it's certainly a bit of a moral dilemma. I think you do have to tell her though."

"Yes. I'd concluded that myself. I really don't want to do any more of these things for other people. It's one thing to discover skeletons in your own family's cupboard but quite another to dig them out of someone else's."

Pete laughed at the mixed metaphor. "Time for me to cook. We're having seafood pasta. You can sit there with a little glass of white wine while I prepare the meal."

After a very pleasant meal, Pete sat down next to his mother and looked her straight in the face. "Now, I hope you don't mind but I've taken a chance and bought tickets for us for tomorrow, without checking with you first. I didn't know whether I'd be able to get them until this afternoon and I didn't want to disappoint you."

"Whatever you've planned I'm sure I'll enjoy it!" said Mitsy.

"A friend of mine has two tickets for the Dublin Racing Festival that she cannot use. She's asked around and I've been waiting to hear if another friend wanted them, as she'd asked him first. I said we'd love to buy the tickets if he doesn't want them."

"So, what exactly is it?"

"Mum!! It's the horse racing meet of the year in Dublin. It takes place at the Leopardstown Racecourse which isn't far at all from here. My friend, Sue, who sold me the tickets, has kindly agreed to give us a lift there. It means we will have to go quite early so she can find somewhere to park. It also means there will be a bit of walking and I wanted to check that you hadn't worn yourself out doing shopping today."

"Oh, that will be lovely. I've never been to a horse race before – that will be fun. Can I bet on the horses?"

"Of course you can. We will give ourselves a budget so we're not tempted to go too mad and I'll get a copy of the Racing Post so we can pick our winners."

"You know I said I'd like to treat us to a meal out tomorrow evening? Will that still be possible?"

"Certainly will. We might be best to book straight away because the city will be busy, it being a Saturday and the Racing Festival."

"Would your friend Sue like to join us?"

"I would think so. She'll be with her friend Maura, so it would be four of us."

"I thought we could go to 'The Old Mill Restaurant' at Temple Bar," said Mitsy, "could you check with Sue and Maura and then book a table for four, please?"

With the arrangements made, there was just time for a mug of cocoa before bed. Again, Mitsy slept extremely well.

She was surprised when her son tapped gently on the bedroom door to wake her up, the next morning. He had already been out to the paper shop for the Racing Post. While Pete was getting breakfast, Mitsy had a look at the paper and remarked, "Ooooh look. There's a horse called A Walk in the Mill". Pete called out from the kitchen, "is that important?"

"Well, it might be Pete. It could be lucky!" she said to herself, under her breath.

He wandered back in with toast and coffee, glancing at the paper on the table. "No, Mum. That article you've just been reading is about a horse that was racing at Aintree recently. It won't be here in Dublin today. Let's have a proper look at today's starters."

They had breakfast together and marked their favoured horses on the paper together. Pete looked at the form, the trainer and the jockey for each horse before he made his selection. Mitsy chose hers on the basis of their names, what she called lucky numbers and the colour of the silks.

The rest of the weekend passed by in a blur of fun and laughter. Mitsy enjoyed the company of Pete's friends Sue and Maura. None of them won much money on the horses, in fact they all spent more than they won, but they didn't mind because the racing was a great spectacle and it was lovely to see other racegoers' joy when their horse came in.

As planned, Sunday was a very easy-going day. They had a short walk in the grounds of Trinity College, enjoying the green space and blue skies. Pete took his mother to one of his favourite pubs and even got her to drink a half of draught Guinness. Pete insisted it was so much better than the bottled version available in England, but Mitsy couldn't tell as she rarely drank anything other than wine and not much of that either.

By eight o'clock when the airport taxi was due, she was well and truly worn out. It had been a wonderful weekend and the memories would stay with her for a long time. Now she was ready to go home and sleep in her own bed. "See how quickly I have accepted Appledore House as my home now," she said to Pete. That, in itself, apart from the great time they had enjoyed, reassured him that he was doing everything he could for his mother.

As her plane landed at Leeds/Bradford, she could see a lone but familiar figure waiting just inside the arrivals lounge. "Good old Mr P, I couldn't ask for more," she thought.

14

Kate was looking forward to Mitsy's return and intended to meet up with her immediately after breakfast on Monday, as she was keen to know what she had discovered during her Dublin trip.

"Come in and sit down," said Mitsy, wondering just how she was going to break the news to her friend.

"First, I'm going to tell you all I've been up to, then we will get the ancestry documents out and I will talk you through my findings. I also want to know if I've missed anything exciting while I've been away."

Kate was all too happy to tell Mitsy that very little had happened at Appledore House during her short absence.

"Oh. There was one thing that was rather sad. Do you know Meg who lives a few doors from me on the first floor?"

"No. I don't think so."

"Well she was taken ill on Friday night and we had an ambulance with its sirens going and blue lights flashing. I've not heard any news, so I don't know if she is better. Or worse."

"I suppose we have to expect this sort of thing, given that we are all getting on a bit. I have to say I really don't like it when people refer to Care Homes like ours as 'God's Waiting Room'. As far as I'm concerned, I'm not waiting for anything. I'm doing my best to live my life to the full, within the constraints of my age and abilities."

After a brief summary of all she did in Dublin, Mitsy realised that she could not put off the difficult part of the conversation any longer.

"Right, Kate. You may find what I have to say rather distressing and I don't want to upset you. Would you like to have a quiet look at this birth certificate and my handwritten notes?"

Kate sat reading for a few minutes and Mitsy noticed that Kate's face slowly drained of all colour, until she was quite pale.

"You don't need to say anything Mitsy. I did have my suspicions but Mam and Dad never talked about my sister and refused to visit her when she lived on the outskirts of Dublin. Then she met an American soldier and she went with him after the war to the USA and we lost touch completely. From your other notes it looks as though she lived in St Louis for many years and only passed away twelve years ago."

They both sat quietly for a while, thinking about the implications. "I'll still think of Mam and Dad as my real parents, because they brought me up. I do wonder who my birth father was though."

Mitsy had thought about this already and decided she really did not want to pursue this line of enquiry herself. "It will probably be impossible to discover Kate. In my opinion, the knowledge could even bring more heartache. "

"Thank you so much Mitsy for your efforts on my behalf. I'm inclined to agree with you, especially as everyone is dead now and it wouldn't do much good raking over the past. Do I owe you some money for what you did?"

"Certainly not, Kate. Changing the subject, would you like to go out for a short walk with me this afternoon? I've discovered a footpath through a small wood and it would be good to have your company."

The two friends hugged each other and arranged to meet after lunch.

That afternoon, the skies cleared and the weather was ideal for a short walk, mild and a little breezy but no problem for two older ladies who were dressed for the outdoors. Mitsy's idea was to give Kate other things to think about so she didn't dwell on the news she had shared with her friend.

"Here it is!" she exclaimed at the beginning of the footpath.

"You are adventurous," said Kate. "I've lived here almost three years and I haven't discovered half the places you have."

The wood itself barely justified the description; it was more like some scrubby bushes where children built their 'camps' within a perimeter of taller trees. Well, it's got us outside anyway, thought Mitsy.

"If it's adventure you're after, perhaps I can tempt you to join me in my next one?"

Kate looked a bit unsure, a facial expression Mitsy was beginning to recognise.

As they walked back, Mitsy pointed out the former Park Mill and the all too obvious For Sale sign outside. She also divulged her evening sightings inside the building. Kate suggested all the explanations Mitsy herself had considered, such as squatters, homeless people, drug dealers etc and Mitsy discounted all of those for one reason or another.

"I have a feeling it's something really exciting, to do with the history of the place," she said. "And I have another discovery, but you mustn't tell anyone this," she said, very softly. "Did you know that there's a room behind the kitchen, where the staff sit when they are on night duty?"

Kate shook her head.

"Well, there's a door that opens to the side of the building that is never locked."

"Is that important?" asked Kate.

"I had this idea, only last night. Suppose that the next time I saw the lights on in the old mill, and you rang your night bell so that whoever is on duty came to check on you and I used the opportunity to creep out the back and go over

71

to the mill to look in the windows? You could just say you had a nightmare or something and keep the carer talking for a few minutes so that I had time to nip back in."

Kate looked very dubious but giggled at the thought of such misbehaviour. Mitsy concluded that the short walk and subsequent conversation had worked its magic as Kate seemed much more relaxed as they rang the front door bell and agreed to see each other at mealtime.

After dinner, a plan was hatched. If (or in her mind, when) she saw lights on in Park Mill, Mitsy would get dressed ready to go out then she would text Kate to initiate the diversionary tactics. After a short pause, Kate would follow instructions and ring the bell for assistance from whichever carer was on duty. Mitsy would already be in place, ready for her excursion to the outdoors as soon as she saw someone heading for Kate's room. Of course, this did depend on Kate hearing her mobile buzz which might be a little unreliable if she was fast asleep. They both giggled to think what an adventure it would be. They also had a back-up plan in case Mitsy got stuck outdoors, so it was essential that she took her mobile with her. What could go wrong?

As luck would have it, that evening Mitsy tried to sleep but she was actually rather excited about their planned escapade. When she got up to check if anything was happening in the Mill, she was rewarded with flickering lights and obvious activity. She was ready and dressed in minutes, with a small torch and her mobile in her pocket. A quick check to make sure things were still happening and then she texted Kate with the pre-agreed message:

Action stations! Wish me luck

She seemed to wait for ever but then Kate replied with a thumbs up. Outside her bedroom Mitsy paused, breathing heavily with excitement. In no time at all she saw Jo heading rapidly for the lift and so she hastened her steps towards the kitchen. She was a little wary in case there was more than one person on night duty but all seemed quiet when she got there.

Mitsy was surprised how easily it had all gone and as she crossed the road, she could still see people moving around in the Mill. Although she wouldn't admit it to Kate, she was really quite nervous.

By the time she reached the nearest window her breathing was close to panting. She stepped forward and looked through the dusty window. It took her several seconds to register what she was seeing and already she was afraid she had been out too long.

With a last glance at the incredible sight, she hurried back across the road, along the side of the building, in the door and closed it behind her. She had merely seconds to spare as Jo came back into the kitchen.

"Oh, hello Mitsy. Is everything OK?"

Mitsy took a deep breath and trying to make her voice sound steady and as normal as possible, she said, "I was thirsty so I thought I would see if I could have a cup of tea but now I've had a drink of water I'm fine so I'll just go back to bed and I'm sorry to trouble you." It all came out in a rush but Jo seemed distracted and didn't notice the cool air in the room from the recently opened door or Mitsy's flushed face and shaking hands.

"That's no problem Mitsy, you go back to bed then."

Back in room 6, Mitsy texted Kate a quick update:

Back safe. Real people in there! C U tomo xx

At breakfast, Kate and Mitsy gave each other a secret smile.

"Did you sleep well, Kate?"

"Oh, I had a bit of a disturbed night but nothing to worry about," she smirked.

"Will you be joining the craft group today?"

"Yes. I was planning to. How about you?"

"I've signed up, although I don't know what we will be making today. Would you call round for me before, say about two o'clock?"

Kate nodded her agreement.

15

"So… what did you see?" asked Kate that afternoon, barely before Mitsy's door was closed behind her.

"Ooooh. Sit down and I'll tell you everything! Well, the first thing I noticed as I crossed the road was that all the ground floor lights were on and I could see shadowy shapes moving inside. As I got closer, I could hear a lot of noise. When I got to a window, I looked in. The glass was really dirty but I could see lots of machines and people moving around. I believe what I saw was when the Mill was fully operational. Honestly you couldn't make it up. I wanted to stay and watch more but I was really aware that you were keeping me safe from discovery so I came straight back. It was in the nick of time because the second I got inside the kitchen door and closed it behind me, Jo came in. I had to make up some excuse about wanting a cup of tea but having a drink of water instead and dashing off to bed. She didn't seem to think it was strange. How did it go for you, Kate?"

"Although I say so myself, I think I did a rather good job of my diversionary tactics. I ruffled my hair so it looked like I had been asleep, threw the duvet around a bit and moistened my eyes to look as if I'd been crying. Then I rang the night bell and when Jo arrived, I tearfully told her I had heard a baby crying. She reassured me that it was highly unlikely but I kept saying how much it upset me. Eventually, I agreed that I may have dreamt it and I 'allowed' her to sit with me until I had settled. I was so relieved when I got your text to say you were back safely."

"Well done Kate. You are quite the little actress, aren't you?! I don't really know what to think about what I saw but it was truly an adventure wasn't it?!"

Looking at her bedside clock, Mitsy could see it was time to go to the craft class, so the pair of them left her room, both grinning like naughty schoolgirls.

Today's craft class was being run by Jeannie again. Mitsy, Kate, Norma and Arthur sat together at one of the round dining tables that Mr P and Greg had set up for the session. Jeannie introduced her topic by explaining that there were lots of sayings to explain what they were about to do. "Many hands make light work" was one of them. They were each going to knit a small square which would be a modest task for each person, then she would stitch them all together to make a blanket for a family in need. After the anticipated chorus of concerns from those who had never knitted a stitch before, Jeannie gave a simple demonstration. She also suggested that each table had at least one person who was not experienced so that the others could help.

Each table was given four pairs of knitting needles and a bag of wool in mixed colours. Mitsy's table got to work straight away. Mitsy knew she'd be slow and Arthur was spending more time dropping his needles and his ball of wool than actually managing to cast on, as Jeannie had shown them. It turned out that Norma had always enjoyed knitting and in South Africa she had been in demand to knit baby clothes for her friends' grandchildren. So Norma kindly started the knitting for Arthur and once underway he was able to finish off the square, although rather slowly. Kate was not especially enjoying the task and as far as Mitsy could see, she was still thinking about their previous night's adventure.

It surprised everyone to see how quickly the small squares grew and one or two people asked if they could knit a second square. "No. I'd prefer it if you gave a friend who's a bit slower than you a helping hand, please," she said.

In this way, the afternoon passed by in pleasant conversation and not a little industry and once again, Mitsy was happy to have found a few friends whose company she could enjoy from time to time.

16

After yet another good night's sleep 'this must be almost a record!', thought Mitsy, it seemed like a good time to get down to some serious ancestry research. Recently she had been distracted by Pete's visit, seeing her sister Sky, the trip to Dublin and a number of enjoyable activities organised by Appledore House.

This time she was planning to look into her father's family tree. Sitting comfortably at her desk, she began by writing down what she knew. Her dad, David Thompson, was born in West Yorkshire in 1913. He married her mother Iris, in 1937, which was the year of the coronation of King George VI and Queen Elizabeth. For most of his life he was a musician, playing folk music initially and later on working as a composer in various music genres. He died in France in 1989.

First, Mitsy was able to track down her dad's birth and death certificates and a couple of census references. The latter were rather random, because of the way they travelled around; they were not exactly of 'no fixed abode' but she suspected that often her parents were not registered anywhere and maybe not even paying tax anywhere! From her father's birth certificate, she could see that his parents were named Herbert and Alice. Herbert was listed as being a trader, although there was no more information than that. She didn't remember her dad ever saying much about his father, or his mother for that matter.

She was beginning to wish that she had a printer in her room, because every time she tracked something down, she had to make a handwritten note of it, in case it led her to something else of interest. It was all rather time consuming and before she knew it, the bell was ringing to signal that residents were being called to the dining room.

She did smile to herself at the relatively easy life she had, now that she didn't have to do the food shopping, meal planning and preparation, not to mention the freedom from washing up. When she lived on her own, it always seemed to Mitsy that the amount of washing up was out of proportion to the size of the actual meal as it appeared on the plate and of course, there was never any surprise regarding what she was going to eat, given that she had prepared it herself. In fact, sometimes after she had gone to a lot of trouble to make herself a meal, she couldn't be bothered to eat it. If it was suitable for freezing, she let it cool and then put it in the freezer for another day. Otherwise she put it in the bin and made herself a cheese sandwich. This didn't happen often because she was careful not to waste food when so many people around the world were starving.

Anyway, self-catering was no longer a problem and she ambled along to the dining room feeling quite cheerful.

Lucy was the only person already in the room, so Mitsy sat down next to her. She hadn't immediately warmed to Lucy so far, partly because of her narrow-minded views about people's skin colour in a previous conversation. Still, I mustn't hold that against her, perhaps she has led a sheltered life and lacks a wider view of the world, she thought. Lucy immediately started chatting and again Mitsy got the feeling that she would not be the kind of person with whom to share a secret.

"Wasn't it awful about poor Meg?" she began. Mitsy shook her head and Lucy immediately assumed that she was aware of the matter and had agreed it was awful. Before she had a chance to say anything, Lucy was already complaining, "I do think they could have done more to help. It's shocking – the state of the NHS today." At this point and before Lucy could continue, Mitsy interrupted, "I'm afraid I'm not up with this news." This was all the invitation Lucy needed and she launched into an explanation about how Meg, who lived on the first floor, was taken ill, rushed to hospital and died of pneumonia.

Mitsy didn't think it was fair to blame the NHS. In spite of all the care and attention of the healthcare team, people did die. Lucy had quite a simplistic view of hospitals where only the doctors were important and she was under no illusion that they had failed in this instance.

Lucy reminded Mitsy, in some ways, of her sister Sky who was always ready to complain about anything. By contrast, friends had often told Mitsy that they loved her sunny personality and optimistic outlook on life. She knew that she generally saw the best in people, although as she got older, she had become less likely to trust others immediately until she was sure of them. I have probably developed more grown-up defence mechanisms, she thought. Anyway, it's best to be wary of Lucy!

Fortunately, several more people arrived in the dining room and Mitsy was able to turn her attention to other topics of conversation. Delicious cooking smells emanated from the kitchen and shortly, bowls of green salad and a serving plate heaped with garlic bread arrived on the table. Finally, everyone received a portion of lasagne.

"Whatever is THIS?" asked Lucy. Mitsy sighed. If she makes one single mention of 'foreign' food I shall be tempted to tip it over her head, she thought. Of course, she didn't, but her patience was being sorely tested. Several people made comments about how lovely and cheesy it was, as well as how authentic. Others referred to wonderful holidays they had enjoyed in Italy. It was enough to deter Lucy from more negative comments so instead she turned to the forthcoming funeral for 'poor Meg'. Mitsy did her best to enjoy her meal whilst discussing across the table with other people some of the current sporting activities which were on the TV.

As soon as they had finished dessert, which was a fresh fruit salad, Mitsy got up and beat a hasty retreat to the sanctuary of room six, making a mental note to avoid sitting next to Lucy in future.

In order to clear her head, she went straight back to her ancestry research. She thought that by concentrating on this, it would stop her feeling irritated by Lucy. From Herbert Thompson, she discovered that his father (that would be Mitsy's great grandfather) was called Frederick David Thompson. He was born in 1868 and at one stage his employment was listed as 'overlooker'. Mitsy made a note of all these things on her handwritten family tree. It was more of a skeleton than a tree, but she was making progress.

Mitsy easily got side-tracked and today was no exception. She decided to search on Google what an overlooker did for a living. Much to her surprise, it seemed to be a supervisory role which was very often carried out in textile mills in the North of England. Feeling that she needed some confirmation of this, as Google isn't always correct, she thought, she phoned Arthur to get his opinion.

Arthur was delighted to be consulted and they talked for some twenty minutes on the phone. It occurred to Mitsy that she could easily have called round to his room, although she still wasn't sure of the visiting etiquette in the Care Home. I'm sure a phone call was best, she said to herself.

With a sigh of satisfaction, she felt she had made progress today and with that, she logged off.

17

Today's outing was by minibus to visit Fountains Abbey, with an optional excursion to Brimham Rocks for those who could tackle some walking. Mitsy knew Fountains Abbey really well, as it was only a short drive from her former home in Harrogate but she had decided, along with Arthur and one or two others, to miss the trip to Brimham Rocks in favour of a snack or light lunch in a café. They were all looking forward to spending time at the famous Cistercian monastery, which was established in the tenth century and set in peaceful and attractive grounds. Fortunately, the day dawned bright and clear, with no hint of rain.

As Mitsy waited for the arrival of their transport at the front of Appledore House, several others joined her. "There always seems to be a builder's skip in the car park here. I wonder why that is?" she commented.

"There's a simple, if sad reason," said Eva. "Whenever someone dies, they redecorate the room."

Mitsy looked a bit puzzled, so Eva explained further. "You know that Meg passed away last week?" Mitsy nodded. "Well, her family came in at the weekend, to take away her clothes and personal belongings. Then Mr P and Greg emptied out the furniture including the mattress. Most of that goes in the skip. The curtains and soft furnishings get washed or dry cleaned then they will redecorate the room this week. In a few days it's all as good as new for the next person to move in. There's quite a waiting list for Appledore House so we should be joined by a new resident within the week."

"Oh, I hadn't thought about that. It makes sense, I suppose," said Mitsy sadly.

By this stage it was well past ten-thirty which was the time that they were asked to assemble. Jo appeared to say that the minibus was on its way and if they were getting cold, they should wait indoors. Just at that moment, the vehicle and its smiling driver hove into view and like schoolchildren they all cheered.

Mitsy and Eva sat next to each other on the coach. This meant that Mitsy had to give her usual explanation of the origin of her name. She also discovered that Eva had signed up for the Brimham Rocks part of the trip and as Mitsy knew all too well, these pre-historic rock formations are most impressive. She was just starting to tell her companion all about them, when Eva interrupted – politely – to say that she was already familiar with the area in general and the Rocks in particular.

"I love Brimham Rocks and I have specified in my will that I would like my ashes to be scattered there."

"Oh, my goodness. I've just updated my will but I didn't think to include that sort of detail for my funeral arrangements," said Mitsy. "In fact, I try not to think much at all about dying!"

"I see what you mean but you know, when someone dies at Appledore House it just reminds you that none of us are here forever."

Mitsy was hoping to move the conversation on to a more optimistic frame of reference and fortunately they were approaching Fountains Abbey, so she recounted some of her happiest outings there with her husband Peter when he was on shore leave and also when Pete was little.

Mitsy was a friendly and thoughtful person but she preferred not to discuss really personal matters with a virtual stranger. It did set her thinking though, and later that morning while walking alone through the Chapel of the Nine Altars she began to reflect on her life and her beliefs.

She did not go to church regularly, except for weddings and funerals, but she did wonder if a higher power (she wouldn't call it God) existed, even though she was quite certain that human life on earth developed through evolution. Somehow it seemed to her that all life, including animals, had a soul or spirit that was part of the essence of a being which continued after their death. This was why she wasn't afraid of the White Lady. She also suspected that the shadowy figures she saw at the old mill were like 'echoes' of people who had worked there in the past.

Her ponderings were cut short when she met up with Arthur, Norma and Kate who had been wandering together in a different part of the grounds. "Isn't it lovely," said Norma. "We've been to see the Water Garden! How about you?"

"I've had a very relaxing stroll around the Abbey and I was just wondering where you three were!" said Mitsy

"Isn't it time we got some lunch?" suggested Arthur.

Kate waved her map at the others. "Let's go to the Mill Café, it's not far."

Mitsy smiled to herself. It seemed that no matter where she went there were reminders of the mill. As well as this latest suggestion, there was "The Old Mill Restaurant" in Dublin where she had spent such a happy evening with her son Pete and his friends Sue and Maura.

Lunch here was a jolly affair, with sandwiches or wraps, cakes and chocolate biscuits and several pots of tea. Just as the four of them were beginning to think they may have outstayed their welcome in the café, the rest of their group appeared, all quite weary but glowing with warmth from their walk.

After another viewing of the main sights of Fountains Abbey and a tour of the gift shop, the four friends headed back to the coach park. Eventually, everyone was reassembled and the after the minibus driver had done a second headcount just to make sure he wasn't leaving anyone behind, they set off for home.

As they drove up the road towards Appledore House, Mitsy observed that a new sign had been erected in front of Park Mill. It said 'ACQUIRED BY' and then a company name in small letters. There were also two men with clipboards standing there. This was enough temptation for Mitsy and as soon as they had all dismounted the minibus, she walked over to where the men were standing. None of her friends noticed she was missing as they filed back into Appledore House.

"Err. Excuse me for being a teeny bit nosey, but can you tell me what is happening to the old Park Mill, please?"

The two men looked rather surprised at this intervention.

"You see, I live over the road at Appledore House and we're all interested to know if there's anything happening," said Mitsy with one of her innocent-looking, girlish smiles.

"Oh. Hello, my dear. The mill is going to be turned into twenty luxury apartments."

"But I thought the planning permission had been turned down?"

"Yes. It had been, but the plans were resubmitted with some changes and it's been accepted now. Do you want to have a look at them?"

"Yes, please. That's very kind of you."

"Well, we do want to get on with our new neighbours!" said the older man of the two.

They spread out the plans on the bonnet of their car and pointed out the changes. Apparently, the main planning reservations were about the availability of parking for future residents. This was to be resolved by clearing an area that was originally identified for two extra apartments.

"You see round the side of the building, here? Well that door, which used to be where the mill workers came in and out, will be the door to the private car park. These old outhouses and sheds will be knocked down and the area will be landscaped and parking spaces will be added. Here, you can see the artist's impression."

"Oh, that looks very nice," said Mitsy. "It will be a benefit to the area, rather than us looking at a derelict building. How soon will the work start?"

"Straight away!" said the other man.

"Thank you so much for your time and explanation. I shall tell my friends the good news." With that she headed back across the road and rang the doorbell to get back in.

Back in room six, Mitsy sat down to gather her thoughts. However, she was destined not to have much time to relax. First, Arthur phoned to tell her that his daughter Jackie was hoping to visit. He wanted the details of the Travelodge where Pete stayed, given that it was convenient for Appledore House. Mitsy was happy to help.

Barely had she put the phone down when it rang again. It was Pete. "Did you get my email, Mum?"

Whatever was Pete phoning for? "No, Pete. I've been out most of the day and only just got back to my room. Is there something wrong?"

"Far from it. We have got a buyer for the house and they want to proceed straight away. The estate agent tells me they are cash buyers, so it's all systems go. I did most of the preparatory work when I was over last but I need to go to the house as soon as possible to oversee the furniture removal. So, I'll be coming over there and calling in to see you, as soon as I get back from this meeting in Finland."

"That's great news Pete. Message me as soon as you know when you'll be here. As it happens, I've just given my friend Arthur the details of where you stay because his daughter Jackie will be visiting. I've been to Fountains Abbey today. It was a lovely outing. Anyway, I must stop nattering. Love you!"

"Love you too Mum. See you soon!"

Mitsy sighed. It was great to see more of Pete at the moment, but of course once all the house business was done, they would probably revert to seeing each other three or four times a year.

Before she had time to check the email that Pete had already told her about, there was a knock at the door. Mitsy sighed again. She actually wanted a little time to herself. It was good to go out and talk to lots of people, but sometimes one just needs a bit of headspace.

It was Kate. "I saw you chatting up those men! What was that about?"

"Come in Kate and I'll tell you," said Mitsy.

Kate sat down and Mitsy gave her a brief summary of the conversation with the developers. She didn't really want to say more until she had thought it through herself.

"Did you enjoy Fountains Abbey?"

"Oh yes. It was just what we needed; a change of scene. By the way, are you coming to the singing tomorrow?"

Mitsy had somehow failed to register that there was a singing group coming up and in fact she must have seemed to be quite confused when she told Kate that she wasn't too keen on singing as she couldn't hold a note. It transpired that it would be a visiting choir calling in to sing for them. Plenty of the residents loved singing but Mitsy found that sort of thing rather patronising so she struggled to find a polite way of declining the invitation.

"Probably not, Kate. I'll see how things are tomorrow."

With that, Kate departed, giving her friend a little hug as she went. Well, she seems to have accepted her family situation anyway, thought Mitsy.

The issues running through Mitsy's mind were quite simple really and this was what she put in her notebook:
- how soon will building works start at Park Mill?
- will the people that I've been watching disappear?
- how do I get just one more visit?
- could I use the workers' side door?
- how to get out of here and back indoors safely?

She didn't have answers to these but in any case, there was another knock at the door. Mitsy closed her notebook and heaved a really heavy sigh this time.

It was Joyce, on her evening medication round.

"Hello Mitsy. How are you doing?"

"I'm fine, thank you Joyce. I'm rather tired as it's been a full day."

"Are these painkillers working alright for you?"

"Oh yes. I prefer not to take them unless I need them. I think after so much walking today, I shall be glad of them."

"I hope you sleep better tonight then Mitsy. Goodnight."

After Joyce left, Mitsy had an idea. She knew that Joyce came to every resident in their room at around the same time every evening. She also knew that she started her room calls downstairs at the far end of the house; in other words, room six. After the ground floor, she went up in the lift and completed the process for upstairs. So…if she sneaked out via the front door or the door behind the kitchen as soon as Joyce had been to see her, she would have at least twenty minutes, maybe even half an hour, to make her exploration of the mill.

She stood for some time at the small window but there was no sign of the flickering lights across the road. Maybe it's stopped already, she thought.

18

Mitsy loved flowers. She especially loved wild flowers. Primroses, violets, celandines and wild garlic all cheered her up, even when it was raining. The sky was grey and the heavens opened not long after breakfast so, although she hadn't intended to, she went along to the lounge where a demonstration of flower arranging was taking place. She had to give the staff of Appledore House credit for setting up so many activities to inspire the imagination of their residents. If I was still living on my own in Harrogate I would be looking out of the windows and wondering what I could do to pass the time of day once all the household chores were done, she thought.

She was also delighted to see that the flower arranger was a man. It pleased her when there were opportunities to challenge people's stereotypes. Of course, there was absolutely no reason why flower arranging should be the purview solely of women. Dave was also pleased to see that the room was filling up and he smiled at Mitsy who took a seat at the front of the room.

That's another thing, thought Mitsy. Why do people tend to head towards the back row? Are they afraid of being asked something? Or learning something? She called it 'naughty children syndrome' in her head and she couldn't resist turning around to see who was sitting in the back row. As she half expected, Lucy was there, along with a couple of other ladies and the three of them were whispering behind their hands.

Dave did ask a few questions, but these were general and not directed at anyone. He just wanted to assess their level of knowledge and experience before he launched into his demonstration.

It was all very interesting and his displays at various levels of complexity were delightful. Mitsy asked him if there was anything that she could have done to preserve the red roses picked from her garden a few weeks ago. They had been lovely at the time but began to drop their petals after a week. Dave helpfully explained about cutting the woody stems on the diagonal, removing any leaves or growth below the water line, refreshing the water, re-cutting them after six days and giving the water a boost by adding soda water or something fizzy.

At the end of the demonstration, Mrs P came into the room to say thank you and everyone applauded Dave politely. Dave had three completed floral displays that he had created as part of the presentation and he kindly handed them to the three people who, in his opinion, had contributed positively to the demonstration. Of course, he didn't say that, as he appeared to hand them out randomly but somehow the recipients, one of whom was Mitsy, knew from Dave's barely perceptible wink, that they had been appreciated. Mitsy noticed that Dave had included a red rose in her vase.

When she got back to her room, Mitsy was surprised to find a message on her phone and an email from Pete.

> Hi Mum! I'm in Bradford! Sorry I couldn't let you know before but I managed to get a late flight direct from Helsinki last night. I've already been over to the house and presided over the furniture removal. All went well. I'll phone later and drop in to see you if I can but it might have to be a quick one. Love Pete xxx

All this apparently sudden activity was disconcerting for Mitsy. She knew her former home had to be sorted out finally but she didn't feel prepared for it today. It was such a shame, as she had really enjoyed the flower arranging demonstration and had felt quite calm and collected when she left.

Thankfully, the rain had stopped so she decided to go for a quiet and solitary walk for twenty minutes in order to rebalance her equilibrium. She noticed that the 'Acquired by' sign outside the Mill had been joined by a further sign announcing the development work, some examples of the interior of the apartments and the artist's impression of the whole site once completed. By the time she had reached the post office and bought some stamps for her next letter to Sky, she had rationalised her feelings.

Just as her old home was almost a closed book to her now, a stage in her life that was over, in the same manner her fascination with Park Mill and its history was also moving into a new chapter. She walked back home, to Appledore House, in a reflective state of mind.

Indoors, a new message was waiting for her from Pete. He was hoping to call in to see his mother around four o'clock, hopefully for a couple of hours.

19

A gentle tap on the door just before four o'clock and Mitsy was amazed to see two people standing there. "Mum, this is Jackie. She's come to see her father. I believe Arthur is a friend of yours?"

Mitsy may have left her mouth open a second too long but she quickly smiled a greeting.

"I've just come up from London to see Dad and when I met Pete in the hotel earlier, he kindly offered to give me a lift. We discovered we had a connection with Appledore House just by chance! It's very good to meet you Mrs Howard. Dad has settled in very nicely, thanks to your kindness towards him."

Jackie smiled at Mitsy, nodded towards Pete then, "See you later, Pete" as if they had known each other for years.

"Come in. Come in and tell me all your news," said Mitsy, nodding towards the cardboard box that Pete was carrying. "What's that?"

Pete refused to say anything until he was actually in his mother's room and sitting down.

"Right. First of all, the house clearance went like a dream. It only took a couple of hours and the men were very careful with everything. I feel confident most of the furniture will go to good homes where the new owners will value it and will appreciate the care you have taken in looking after it over the years. The house clearance company will put some money into my account electronically and in due course I will pass it on to you."

This was more or less what Mitsy was expecting. "Pete, dear. I'd rather you keep the money; you've done all the organisation and given up your time to sort it out. I don't need it."

"Well, thank you Mum, if you say so. OK so, next bit of news, is that the house sale is going through just nicely. It will take time and at the moment the buyers are waiting for their surveyor's report. I suppose they might try to knock down the price on the basis of the findings. On the other hand, I know the couple are in rented accommodation and keen to get moved in before school term starts as the husband is starting a new job as deputy head teacher nearby."

Again, Mitsy nodded. Frankly she couldn't care less as long as the sale went through now. Everything to do with the house seemed a long way in the past.

"Right. This is the exciting bit! I did a last check round the house before the removers arrived and I found this box in the dark tucked right at the back of the cupboard under the stairs. I don't know how much you know about what grandad did when they first lived in the house?"

"He wrote music, played a bit and he used to go down to London a lot, I believe."

"What I found in this box is really interesting. At that time, probably when you were children, music used to be recorded live and captured on a wax master disk. That was then transferred to a metal electroform and to make multiple copies they stamped it with some sort of shellac material. That was in the pre-vinyl days, which started in the early 1950s. So, what I'm showing you here are some of grandad's early recordings."

They both looked through the box although nothing actually listed David Thompson on it until they got to the bottom, where there were several reel-to-reel cassettes with his name on.

"I believe when he went to London, he used to go to Alexandra Palace, playing his original score with an orchestra and that was where the recordings were made."

"Now you see, I'm not very well-informed about this sort of thing but it turns out that Jackie, Arthur's daughter, is somewhat of an expert! She works at the BFI (British Film Institute) Archive in North London, well Berkhamsted in Hertfordshire to be precise. She thinks they will have recordings of that film music that grandad was supposed to have written."

"It wasn't 'supposed' Pete, he did write it," rejoined Mitsy, "although I just cannot remember the name of the film. He wrote the music for some radio programmes too."

"Well, I'm meeting up with Jackie later and, if you agree, she will take these precious originals back to work with her where they can properly research what they are, when and where they were produced. It might mean that we will ultimately donate them to the BFI Archive. How do you feel about that?"

Mitsy reassured Pete that she was happy for Jackie and her colleagues to take them. She was also privately rather intrigued how quickly this friendship had sprung up between her son and Arthur's daughter. She convinced herself that it was, probably, no more than a happy coincidence that they had met.

"So, is everything all right then?" said Pete. "Have you signed the new will yet?"

"No. I haven't seen it. Shall I phone Mrs Reed the solicitor?"

Pete said he would chase it up once he got back to Dublin. Mitsy thought she was perfectly capable of phoning herself but decided not to argue.

They sat comfortably together for half an hour or so. Mitsy was on the verge of telling him what she had discovered about his great-grandfather and what was happening at Park Mill, but decided in the end that it would be wisest to keep that to herself for now. She entertained Pete by recounting the things they had made in the craft

94

group and describing the outings. She may have exaggerated just a little bit, but only to make him laugh.

Looking at his watch, "Well, I shall pop upstairs to see if Jackie is ready, as I'm taking her back to the hotel. I thought we might have dinner together this evening. Oh, and I must take that box with me. You take care Mum. Love you!" and with that he dashed off.

It was years since she had seen Pete so animated.

20

After a remarkably good night's sleep, Mitsy was ready to face the day. She had made another appointment with the local hairdresser because she had been too busy to look into alternatives. However, she had promised herself she would try to give a more explicit description of what she wanted done to her hair this time.

Norma had asked if she could walk with her as far as the salon, so that she had a bit of exercise and the opportunity to size up the hairdresser and her clientele in order to decide whether to take the plunge herself. She was still feeling the cold, even though it was growing milder by the day.

Mitsy enjoyed chatting with Norma and so often discovered something new that she had not been aware of previously. Today was no different.

"I am really appreciating having all my clothes washed and ironed at Appledore House," said Mitsy. "Do you know, they even sewed a missing button on my blouse yesterday!"

"I can't say I noticed," said Norma. "I've been used to having the washing done for me most of my life. We always had a laundry boy."

"Oh. Isn't that unacceptable these days – I mean, using them like a slave?"

"Well. It's not quite like that Mitsy. Often, it's the only way the boys can earn some money. You have to bear in mind that with the temperatures being what they are, we need a complete change of clothes every day, if not more frequently, so there's a lot to do. I can see you might think it strange, but if you think about the British habit of paying schoolgirls to babysit their children it is not so very different."

"Yes, I see. I do love learning about these things. Are you still missing your home, Norma?"

Norma thought for a moment then said, "Not as much as I feared. I was actually quite lonely in Port Elizabeth although I didn't realise it at the time."

They approached the hair salon and Norma looked at the window displays, consulted the price list and nodded. "This will do for now. I'll come in with you and make an appointment then I will wander back at my own pace. 'See you later!"

Mitsy had cleverly done an online search of Hair magazine and taken a screenshot of her preferred style. She showed this to the hairdresser who seemed to think she could recreate the cut on Mitsy. As it turned out, it was not too bad at all and Mitsy hurried back to Appledore House with a spring in her step. She had absolutely no reason whatsoever to hurry, but somehow it was a habit that she had not yet discarded now that so many things were being done for her.

The afternoon was spent dealing with what she called 'admin'. There was a large brown envelope in the post, which was the draft of her new will. This meant she had to email Pete to tell him he didn't need to contact the solicitors. Then she had to ascertain whether Mr P would be willing both to witness her will, as well as taking her over to Harrogate to conclude the matter. Then she had to confirm to the solicitor, Mrs Reed, that she was happy with the wording and to book an appointment for herself and Mr P at the solicitor's office. By the time she had spent twenty minutes looking for Mr P, who wasn't actually hiding down the garden, but who was difficult to track down amongst the shrubs, it was almost time for dinner.

Mitsy observed to herself that she had enjoyed every single meal since arriving at Appledore House. Today's was no exception as it was steak and kidney pie. The puff pastry was light and flaky, the meat was tender and smothered in tasty gravy. The modest portion of fresh mixed vegetables was just enough to provide contrast without her feeling too full by the end of the meal. For once she declined the dessert as she thought she had eaten enough and she was being careful not to put on weight, which she suspected would be all too easy to do here.

Back in her room, Mitsy watched a natural history programme on the television. As night fell, she couldn't resist a quick peep across the road. She wasn't surprised to see the lights on inside the Mill and shadows moving past the windows.

At that moment, Joyce tapped on the door to room six. "Hello Mitsy. Excuse me being in a bit of a rush this evening as I've got an important appointment immediately after I've done the meds round!"

Mitsy raised her eyebrows in question. "It's my grand-daughters' ballet show and I promised not to be late."

"Have fun then Joyce. Thank you."

Even as she was saying these words and closing the door behind Joyce, a thought entered her mind. This would be an ideal opportunity to check out the Mill. 'I can nip out of the main door while Joyce is giving out the medication to the residents upstairs and after a carefully timed visit to the mill across the road, I can creep back in via the kitchen door,' she thought.

Patting her coat pockets to check that she had a torch in one, her mobile phone in the other and a scarf wrapped across her face against the night air, Mitsy locked her room door very quietly behind her, slipping the key in her trouser pocket.

She was really excited and aware that with the developers starting work soon, it would probably be the last chance to learn more about the happenings at Park Mill.

As she tip-toed past Norma's room, she could hear Joyce's voice so she strode along with some urgency, around the corner and directly ahead to the front door of the Home. She gritted her teeth as she closed the door behind her with a click, concerned lest anyone heard her exit. Outside, she walked across the gravel, trying hard not to let her footsteps scrunch until she reached the road. There was no traffic, so she was able to cross easily, checking her watch as she went.

21

Mitsy was trying very hard to remember the layout of the building from the plans that the developers had shown her. Once she was past the street lights it was extremely dark, so her torch came in handy. She knew that there was a door at the side of the building, which was previously the main entrance and exit for the workers.

By the time she had reached this, she could see some people standing by the door. Quite afraid, she walked forward, but no one seemed to notice her. She stepped up to the door and, as a woman left the building she slipped inside. Mitsy noticed that there were lights all along this corridor but they were quite feeble. She walked further into the building and just ahead of her were two women hurrying along and talking. They appeared not to see her either and as she got closer to them, she could just make out some of their whispered words:

"What's wrong with Dottie?"

"She's in the family way. Old Thompson again, I believe."

"Oh no. Poor thing. I wonder how she'll manage?"

As they entered the main area of the mill, Mitsy was suddenly deafened by the noise and almost overcome by the smell. The women took up their stations at the looms and began to handle the cotton strands, quite expertly to Mitsy's eyes. The thread ran from floor to ceiling and someone was checking the bobbins to make sure they didn't run out, she presumed.

She could now understand why the women finished their hasty conversation because speaking was out of the question here. The smell was another matter. It was a combination of heat, oil and cotton dust. Mitsy found it hard to breathe. She stood silently by the wall, observing this hive of activity.

There was so much going on that it was hard to think clearly. All she could surmise was that somehow, much as she had suspected, she had been transported back to the time when Park Mill was operating.

She could see at least a dozen women at work, and one man. She was thankful that there were no children, although she knew from her research several weeks earlier that juveniles were employed as apprentices.

The man was striding up and down and from time to time he pointed at one of the women and gestured for her to move to another work station. I suppose he's an overlooker, thought Mitsy.

He had quite a sour-looking face, a dark moustache and a mop of unruly black hair. Mitsy thought that she wouldn't want to meet his sort in a dark alley.

Suddenly there was a bit of commotion half way down the room, but Mitsy decided she should stay where she was. Even if people couldn't see her, she might get in the way.

The overlooker strode down very close to where she stood and shouted and jabbed his finger at the worker nearby. Mitsy could see her blush and shake slightly. Although Mitsy couldn't hear what was said, she could read her lips:

"I'm very sorry Mr Thompson. It won't happen again, I promise."

Suddenly, Mitsy realised she had been gone for quite a while and in any case, she wasn't really happy watching people work under these conditions. At one level it was fascinating, like watching a history lesson using virtual reality but, being the sensitive soul that she was, it was disturbing to see how people lived and worked in these days. She left the big room and quickly headed back down the long corridor that she had followed on her way in, with the cacophonous sounds and polluted air gradually receding.

There was no one near the door, so she turned the handle and left the building almost as quickly as she had arrived. The whole experience had been quite unsettling and with hindsight she wasn't sure what she had achieved apart from satisfying her curiosity.

Outside, she realised that it was raining heavily. She put her head down but before she reached the road there was a flash and a great clap of thunder. Mitsy nearly jumped out of her skin. 'That's guilty conscience for sure,' she said to herself.

Hurling herself across the road and then the gravelled parking area in front of Appledore House, Mitsy realised she was already drenched and she almost broke into a sprint round the side of the building to the secret door behind the kitchen. Turning the door handle, she discovered that it was closed. Even worse, it seemed to be locked.

By now, Mitsy had thoroughly frightened herself. 'You foolish woman. What do you think you are doing?' she said to herself.

Trying to calm herself with deep breaths as the wind blew ferociously around the Care Home, with shaking hands she dug into her pocket for her mobile phone. Thankfully it was still there.

'Well it's a good job I'd put Kate's number on speed dial,' she thought. 'Kate. Kate. Wake up and answer the phone please!'

It seemed like an age before she heard a confused voice say, "What's happening? Who is it?"

"Kate. It's me. Mitsy. I'm locked outside!"

"Outside where?"

"Kate. I'm near the front door. Can you come down and let me in?"

There was a mumbled response which Mitsy had to hope was some form of agreement.

Meanwhile, she stood at the door getting wetter and wetter. Her hair was hanging in rats' tails and she was shivering with cold and not a little fear. Mitsy knew that her behaviour had been somewhat reckless and she was already feeling embarrassed and contrite.

22

The door opened and Kate appeared in her dressing gown with a grave expression all over her face. A few steps behind stood Mrs Podsiadlo.

"Come in Mitsy," said Kate. "Are you OK?"

"Thank you very much Caitlin," said Mrs P. "I'll take over from here. Thank you for your help. Now please go straight back to bed and don't worry, you can talk to Mitsy in the morning."

Mrs P steered Kate back towards the lift. Meanwhile, she gave a serious look to Mitsy. "You, my dear, are coming upstairs with me so that we can get you dry and warmed up."

With that, she took Mitsy's freezing cold hand and led her up the grand staircase and into the Podsiadlo's apartment.

"Right. Take that soaking wet coat off and hang it over there," she directed. As Mitsy was doing as she was told, Mrs P left the room and returned carrying a clean, fluffy and warm towel.

"You can start by drying your hair carefully. There are some tissues over there. Please dry your eyes and sit down by the fire."

Mitsy shivered with cold and fear. What had she done? Would she be asked to leave Appledore House, just as she was beginning to feel settled in? The situation reminded her of her schooldays of long ago, standing outside the headmistresses' room waiting to be told off for some misdemeanour or other. Not that it happened often, but when she did manage to get into trouble it was usually because of a spectacular mishap.

Mrs Podsiadlo, in her pink candlewick dressing gown, came back into the cosy living room with a glass of something in each hand.

"Now, have you dried your hair properly?" she asked, just like Mitsy's mother did when she was a little girl.

"Right. Sit down and have a sip of this." Mitsy gratefully took a sip of the dark liquid and discovered that it was a good quality cognac. So good, in fact, that it almost took her breath away.

"First things first. Perhaps you will explain to me why you were outside, in a thunderstorm, in the middle of the night?" she sounded really severe and Mitsy started to cry again.

After blowing her nose loudly she took a deep breath and, not quite sure where to start, she began in the middle. "I wanted to see inside Park Mill before they started the building works, Mrs Podsiadlo."

"Hmm. Please call me Hannah this evening, given that the circumstances are extraordinary. So, let's try this another way. Why did you want to go to the old mill building in the middle of the night?"

"Well. Ever since I moved to live here at Appledore House, I have been bad at sleeping. No. That's not true. I have always been bad at sleeping. It's just that I could see people in the Mill at night."

Mitsy paused, as if that was all the explanation was needed.

"I see," said Mrs P, who clearly didn't see anything at all and was hoping that the confusion would be cleared up soon. She too, was quite a light sleeper and when she heard the lift operating so late, she went to investigate. Kate was half awake and in quite a state, thinking that Mitsy was in mortal danger, so Mrs P asked her just to open the door calmly and let her take over from there.

105

"So, you saw people in the mill at night? Was that like the ghost you said that you saw here in the house?"

Mitsy began to feel extremely uncomfortable, as if her word was being doubted. She took another sip of her brandy and the warm fluid began to calm her.

"I am sorry Mrs P. Hannah. Yes. I did see shadows of people moving around over the road in the mill. I did an internet search and found out a bit of the history of the place. It was called Park Mill and it was built in the late 19th century. It was a highly productive textile mill which brought prosperity to the area, mainly to the mill owner's family. The workers were not treated well by today's standards, I'm sad to say."

Mitsy paused to gather her thoughts, recognising that she hadn't been exactly coherent up till now.

"Anyway, I've been seeing people moving around in the building for weeks now, but only at night. One day the developers were outside and I had a chat with them. They showed me the plans and how the new apartments were going to be designed. They said the work was starting imminently."

Mitsy wisely omitted to mention that she had already sneaked out through the door behind the kitchen and implied that this excursion was her first foray across the road.

"I thought that if I was going to see who was in the Mill, I needed to do it sooner rather than later. I am very sorry that I didn't really think about the consequences."

"Indeed, you didn't. I dread to think what would have happened if you had tripped on a loose floorboard or something. You could have been trapped there. Did Caitlin know where you were?"

Mitsy realised that she needed to be careful if she wasn't to implicate her friend.

"Oh no. Kate had no idea. I'm just thankful that I had my phone with me and I was able to wake her up."

"And now we have an explanation, of sorts, as to why you were out of doors and going for a walk in the dead of night in a thunderstorm, was the risk worth it Mitsy?"

Mitsy was in fact asking herself the same question, much as she was trying to decide how to answer. Should she tell Mrs P exactly what she saw, or would she think that she had 'lost her marbles'?

Fortunately, and very much in the nick of time, Mr Podsiadlo tapped on the door of his own living room to ask if everything was all right.

"Yes, thank you Antoni. I think we are just about finished here. Mitsy, it's time you went off to bed and I shall arrange for you to have breakfast in your room tomorrow. Well, today, as it is already tomorrow. Try to get some sleep and put this behind you."

"Thank you very much. I am sorry for the trouble I've caused and I promise never to do anything like this again," said Mitsy as she scooped up her coat which was still soaking wet.

23

Whether it was the relief of being rescued, the warmth of Mrs P's electric fire, the cognac or the comfort of her own bed, but Mitsy slept like the proverbial log and woke up feeling more refreshed than she had done for a long time. Breakfast in her room also seemed like quite a treat and absolved her from any early morning explanations. By ten-thirty she had just put on her purple dress, a little make-up and a spritz of her favourite perfume when there was a gentle tap on the door. It was Mrs P. "How are you feeling this morning, Mitsy?"

"Thank you, Mrs P, I am feeling just fine. Can I apologise again for my thoughtless behaviour last night? I assure you it won't happen again."

"No more apologies necessary Mitsy. I just wanted to be sure you were feeling better."

"Thank you. I don't think I have told you properly how happy I am here at Appledore House. I could never have imagined how comfortable I could be - but I am!"

"I'm pleased to hear it. Now I expect you have some explaining to do to Caitlin. I suggested she shouldn't disturb you until elevenses when Jo will be bringing two mugs of coffee to your room."

"Thank you. That will be lovely."

Mitsy had barely closed the door to Mrs P when her phone rang. It was Arthur. "Now then, Mitsy. I'm not being nosey but I just wanted to make sure that you are alright. There was a bit of chatter over the breakfast table suggesting that you had gone 'walkabout' last night and I was feeling concerned for you."

"Thank you, Arthur, you are very kind and I can assure you that I'm fine. I will tell you about it privately some time when I have made sense of everything myself. In the meantime, I would appreciate it if you said nothing to stimulate the rumour mill." Mitsy chuckled to herself silently when she realised exactly what she had said. Why did everything keep reminding her about the mill?

"Also, I just wanted to tell you my little bit of news although I suppose it is no more than gossip and rumour just between us!" he said mysteriously.

"Ooooh. Do tell," she replied.

"You see, I was telephoning my Jackie yesterday. I usually phone her once a week, or she phones me. It turns out that your Pete has just spent the weekend at my Jackie's flat in London. Jackie was very casual about it and implied that it was a business matter. She said that he had just dropped in on his way back from a meeting somewhere. I'd have thought no more about it, except that she mentioned they had been to an art gallery together, had a meal out and a walk in the park. I have to say it sounded like a proper weekend's socialising. What pleased me so much was that Jackie sounded really happy and animated. You know that she was very downhearted when her marriage broke up and it's lovely to hear her sounding happy again. What do you think?"

Mitsy realised that Arthur was quite quick to put two and two together and she didn't want him to be disappointed.

"Well. They did have a genuine reason to meet, which I'll have to explain to you another time Arthur because there's a knock at the door which is likely to be Kate. I'm delighted that Pete and Jackie are getting on well. I'll catch up with you later and thank you for phoning."

In fact, there hadn't been a knock at the door, but Mitsy just felt she needed to think a lot of things through before she spoke to Arthur again.

Kate arrived shortly after, keen to know all about Mitsy's exploits of the previous night.

Mitsy gave her roughly the same summary as she had given to Mrs P, while they drank their coffee. Kate wasn't going to let her off so easily though.

"So…. What did you see there?"

"Well Kate, in some ways I wish I hadn't seen it. Fundamentally I saw the mill as it was being run as a textile mill in the late 19th century. The conditions were appalling, the smells, the dust and the deafening noise. The workers were not being treated well. It was really unpleasant."

"But what did they think of you? Surely it was strange to have someone from the 21st century amongst them?"

"That was what was odd. No one seemed to see me or be aware of me. I just stood and watched."

"And why did you phone me in the middle of the night?"

"Oh Kate. I am really sorry about that. I do apologise and I will never do anything like that again. You see, I left by the front door while Joyce was doing the evening medication round. All was well at that stage and I thought I'd come back in by the 'secret' door behind the kitchen. Anyway, I probably lost track of time because I suddenly realised I'd been gone too long. I left the mill quickly, only to discover we were in the middle of a massive thunderstorm. The rain was pelting down and the thunder and lightning were quite impressive – well, it would have been impressive to anyone who was safe and dry indoors! I hurried back, only to find that the secret door was closed and locked. I got drenched trying to figure out how to get back in. Eventually I concluded that you were my only hope. Thank goodness I had my phone with me!"

"I was deep asleep so it took me a while to grasp what was happening. Was Mrs P very cross?"

"Actually, she was really kind once she had told me off good and proper. I think when you got in the lift to come down to let me in, the clanking sounds must have woken her. She made sure I didn't get chilled and of course she wanted to know what it was all about. Kate, I didn't tell her I saw any people in there – you won't tell anyone will you, please?"

Kate hugged her friend and assured her that she wouldn't say anything. "I was only concerned that you were OK, Mitsy. When Mrs P sent me back to bed last night, I couldn't sleep for worrying about you."

"I am fine, thank you. Something that has puzzled me though, is that while I was there, I overheard two women talking and they had some unpleasant things to say about the supervisor. It seems he had got a girl called Dottie pregnant and from the way it was discussed I don't think she was the first one. A bit later, the supervisor (who was called an overlooker in those days), shouted at another lady worker and she apologised to him by name."

"Well, you said it was an unpleasant environment, Mitsy, so it's not that surprising."

"Yes, but she called him Mr Thompson!!"

"So?"

"When I was searching my family tree, I discovered a Frederick Thompson. He was from this area and he was an overlooker. It's a bit of a coincidence, isn't it? He wasn't very nice. I'm not sure I want him to be my ancestor."

"Oh Mitsy. Whilst I understand that you find this ancestry search fascinating, you know from my situation that one doesn't always find good news or happy stories. I think your advice to me at the time is valid here. Probably best to leave it alone."

The two women sat watching Greg busy at work in the garden and the antics of some birds collecting twigs for their nests, then Kate said, "Right Mitsy. I've satisfied myself that you are none the worse for your escapade, so I shall leave you in peace. I hope you will give up your adventures for now! By the way, have you looked out of your window this morning?"

Mitsy was a bit puzzled as they had been looking out of the window for at least ten minutes, until it occurred to her that Kate meant the other one. Jumping up, the pair of them dashed over to the window that looked out at the mill. There, for all to see, was a team of men erecting a high fence around Park Mill. It was solid, so that people would not be able to see inside, while the works were being carried out.

"You were right on one thing, Mitsy. If you hadn't visited the mill last night you would have missed the opportunity all together."

24

Before going to dinner that evening, Mitsy had been frightened that all the other residents would want to question her about the previous night. Whilst Kate was fully aware and would keep it secret and Arthur may have had some inkling of what it was about, everyone else would be agog with curiosity. She decided that she would pretend that it was an episode of sleepwalking and would keep her fingers crossed that no one challenged her.

As it turned out, anything to do with the night before was entirely forgotten because of the latest happenings. Antoni Podsiadlo had been taken ill that afternoon and had been rushed to the Bradford Royal Infirmary with a suspected stroke.

Mitsy was struck with remorse. Maybe if he hadn't had a disturbed night because of her antics, this wouldn't have happened.

The meal was a sober affair as all the staff had been affected; they were fond of Mr P and really upset. The dinner table conversation amongst the residents was all about how kind and helpful Mr P had been. Mitsy didn't like the way they were talking about him in the past tense; at this stage no one knew if he would recover. However, she thought it best to keep a very low profile and say nothing.

Julie and Sam had been on kitchen duty and had done their best to make a pleasant meal. The chicken curry was tasty enough and the rice had been cooked to perfection, neither hard nor too soft. Dessert was bakewell tart and again, Sam's efforts were rewarded with praise.

As soon as she had finished her dessert, Mitsy rose from the table and Arthur appeared by her side. "May I speak with you, Mitsy?" he asked.

"By all means, Arthur. Would you like to come to my room where we can talk?"

The two walked together along the corridor without speaking, until they were inside room six.

"Sorry to nab you like that Mitsy, but I really wanted to be sure for myself how you are."

Mitsy smiled at Arthur's solicitude. It's a long, long time since anyone has looked after me like that, she thought. Apart from Pete, that is.

"Let's sit down, Arthur. I don't have much to offer you to drink, but I do have a bottle of Stones ginger wine?"

"That would be lovely thank you. I haven't got around to offering hospitality in my room yet. So, what actually happened?" said Arthur, straight to the point.

They clinked glasses before Mitsy began her explanation.

"As you know, Arthur, I have been interested in the derelict mill across the road. I discovered from the internet and also the local paper that it was a busy textile mill, back in the late 19th century and has recently been sold for development into luxury apartments. I have also been puzzled by the fact that most nights, but not always, I have been able to see dim lights on inside the building and shadows which looked like people moving."

Mitsy paused to take a sip of her ginger wine and a deep breath before she continued.

"I had a sneaky look through the windows one night when Kate helped me leave the building. I came back in, after my brief peep, via a secret door at the side of Appledore House which only the staff knew about."

Arthur raised his eyebrows but decided it was best not to interrupt Mitsy's flow of conversation.

"Then I spoke to the developers who were out in the road checking arrangements for the work - it was after we got back from our outing to Fountains Abbey - and they showed me the recently agreed plans for Park Mill. They said the building work was starting imminently."

"Well, I now realise I didn't think things through properly but I went out last night and actually walked over to the mill and then I went inside the building. It was a revelation because they were operating exactly as I imagined they would have been in the past. I saw the bobbins loaded with cotton, the heavy machines and the workers. It was noisy, dirty and back-breaking work."

"Didn't they wonder who you were or what you were doing there?" asked Arthur.

"It's funny as that's exactly what Kate asked. Arthur, I've told no one except you and Kate, you won't tell anyone else, will you?"

Arthur assured Mitsy that he would keep her story confidential.

"So, anyway, no one noticed I was there. They kind of looked through me."

"I saw and heard things that I didn't expect and then I realised I had been gone a long time and came home. Except there was a massive thunderstorm, I got drenched and I was locked out!"

"Oh, Mitsy. You really should be more careful," said Arthur. "How did you get back in?"

"I had to phone Kate. She opened the door but Mrs P was there too. I got a right telling off, I must say. I'm so worried because I must have woken Mr P and now he's been taken ill. It's my fault."

Mitsy was close to tears so Arthur got up to put his arm round her in a reassuring hug. "Now, I'm sure that's just an unfortunate coincidence Mitsy and you mustn't worry about that."

"It's not the only coincidence, Arthur. In the mill, the man who was the supervisor was called Mr Thompson and he was nasty and got girls pregnant and on my internet search I found that on my dad's side of the family there was a man with the same surname and he was an overlooker in Bradford too."

Arthur smiled wryly. "Look, that's the least of your concerns. I'm sure there were many overlookers called that in the mills round here. Thompson is a local name."

Mitsy sighed. "Mrs P was very kind to me once she'd told me off. I really shouldn't have been meddling in something I don't understand."

"If you want my opinion, which you didn't ask for I know, it's time you took a break from your ancestry searching and your unaccompanied visits to old buildings!"

Mitsy looked sadly at Arthur. "But it's my hobby!"

"Couldn't you find a different one, Mitsy?"

She sighed again. "Well, I suppose so. I always planned to write a book when I retired. Maybe I could do that now…"

Part II

One Year Later

Her day had started off with a number of happy surprises, beginning with the delivery of several birthday cards from family and friends, which was followed by the arrival of a beautiful bouquet of a dozen yellow roses sent by Pete via the local florist. Mitsy did so appreciate the effort made by her son to remember her birthday and other special days. No matter where he was in the world, he didn't forget his mother.

She dressed with care, as she always did, on the basis that once an older person lets their appearance slip, it was invariably a downward slope into downright sloppiness. Today was no exception and she got pleasure from wearing the bright cerise dress that she had bought on a shopping trip to Dublin last year, a matching navy jacket with pink piping round the collar and a pretty scarf tied neatly at her neck. She even wore earrings, even though putting them on had taken ten minutes and quite a lot of cursing under her breath!

Meeting Arthur by the front door for their weekly outing to the Standsfield Arms, Mitsy was somewhat taken aback to find that she was being carefully re-directed into the lounge, where virtually everyone from Appledore House was assembled.

She looked around the room and thought how lovely it was that her friends had gone to the trouble of organising a birthday party for her. She didn't remember telling anyone other than Arthur that it would be her 80th today, so it was a genuine surprise. She smiled to think of all the friends she had made since moving in.

Dear Norma, her next-door neighbour, was there. She hadn't lost her South African accent but she had more or less adjusted to the cooler Yorkshire climate. She was great company for outings or just sitting with at mealtimes. Since the first knitting group they had attended, Norma had diligently knitted square after square for the blankets to be sewn together by Jeannie. Family members of other residents even brought in spare wool for her. Mitsy admired her dedication but still couldn't understand the appeal of the craft herself.

The twins, Mandy and Anne, were always entertaining. They had been at Appledore House for several months now and, in spite of their age, were still up to playing pranks on each other. The pair had never married, although for much of their lives they had gone their separate ways, so it was rather a bonus when Mandy decided she didn't want to live alone anymore that Anne agreed to move in too. Anne's room was on the ground floor, because she had some mobility problems and Mandy was upstairs. They were not identical twins, but they did look very alike.

Mandy had been able to take over Eva's old room, which was just what she wanted. Sadly, Eva had passed away in her sleep a few months ago. Mitsy missed her gentle presence but was pleased to discover that her ashes had been taken to Brimham Rocks by her niece, as she had requested.

As she glanced round the room, Mitsy saw that virtually all the residents and most of the staff were there. Lucy hadn't changed much and was contributing to the party atmosphere by telling jokes. As Mitsy suspected she would not be especially amused by them, she stayed the other side of the room and just smiled and nodded.

One of the significant changes during the past year was that Hannah and Antoni Podsiadlo had finally retired from the running of the Home. Antoni had recovered from his stroke, after some timely intervention by the paramedics followed by physiotherapy. Hannah was beginning to show a few signs of early stage dementia so it seemed a good time to take it easy after all those years of caring for others. Maggie had been appointed as Matron and Greg took on all the gardening and house maintenance, assisted by his son Alan. Mr and Mrs P rarely came down from their rooms, so Mitsy was especially appreciative of their appearance today.

Raymond, her neighbour, smiled across the room as he tipped an imaginary hat to her. He had at last started to come 'out of his shell' and was even to be found at breakfast most days. He remained relatively quiet and courteous and all the newcomers loved him.

Then there was Kate, smiling broadly. She was, and always would be, Mitsy's best friend. Apart from her role in Mitsy's escapades, they both knew things about each other that no one else knew, which probably had a played a part in cementing the friendship. She had fully accepted the information that Mitsy had revealed about her parentage some twelve months ago and the subject was rarely mentioned again.

Arthur had become a reliable and special friend too. Every Wednesday lunchtime, Mitsy and Arthur made the short walk up the road to the Standsfield Arms for something to eat and a drink. They had become more adventurous over time because, although the ploughman's lunch was delicious 'well, we don't want to get stuck in a rut, do we?' said Mitsy. Peter the dog was usually in front of the fire before they arrived these days, except in the warmer weather when they sometimes sat in the beer garden.

This was how Arthur was able to set up the birthday get together because Mitsy just thought they were going out for their usual Wednesday lunch. Everyone was invited and only a few residents were unable to be there for one reason or other.

Among the staff who were there, some of whom were not on duty but had called in anyway, were Maggie, Sally, Julie, Jo, Joyce, Ruth, and young Sam. Greg could not be persuaded to come in from the garden as he was not comfortable with anything remotely formal, much as he was fond of Mitsy.

Arthur tapped a spoon on the side of a glass to get everyone's attention. "Hello, everybody. I'm sure you don't need me to remind you that it is Mitsy's birthday today. She won't tell me how old she is and I'm too much of a gent to ask, so we won't be giving her the bumps!" Mitsy smiled because of course Arthur knew exactly how old she was. "In a few minutes we will ask her to cut the birthday cake, but in the meantime please raise your glasses to wish Mitsy many happy returns along with health, wealth and everything she might wish for!"

Everyone clinked glasses and chorused their good wishes. There was a lull in the conversation and although she hadn't had a chance to think it through at all, Mitsy found herself making an impromptu speech.

"Thank you, Arthur and all my dear friends. What a lovely surprise. Little did I think, some eighteen months ago, how happy and contented I would be living here at Appledore House. To be honest, I was really quite nervous to make such a big change in my life, having lived in my home in Harrogate for more than seventy years! This place, and all the people here - that's staff and residents – have been a joy to know and I do hope we all have many more happy years together."

She sat down to lots of applause and Arthur appeared with a large knife with which to cut the cake. Of course, he knew she wouldn't be able to cut it herself, given what she liked to call 'my badly behaved hands', so as soon as everyone turned back to their conversations, Arthur discretely attempted the task himself.

After the party, Mitsy spent almost an hour in the garden, peacefully watching the birds and talking to Greg. She may well have delayed his gardening plans, but like most of the other staff members he believed that conversation with the residents was almost as important as getting jobs done. The pruning would wait for another day.

26

Thursday dawned bright and clear, so Mitsy decided she would get what she called her 'admin' done in the morning and perhaps go for a short walk in the afternoon.

First, she wrote a short note to thank Pete for the beautiful flowers and to tell him about her surprise birthday party. She actually wasn't sure which country he was in, but he always managed to pick up his emails.

Then she accessed her online bank account. After the house was sold last year, and all the solicitor's fees and taxes paid, Pete had deposited a considerable sum of money in savings for Mitsy. They had worked out how much was needed for her monthly payment to Appledore House over the year, and how much she would need for spending money for twelve months. Pete had also added a little more for any contingency such as his mother's laptop expiring. That sum was then transferred to Mitsy's account so that she could manage her finances herself.

Once a month, Mitsy checked that the Appledore House payment had gone through. Of course, it always did but she preferred to check herself. Then she calculated how many things she had bought online and deducted the total from her monthly spending budget.

It wasn't exactly a time-consuming task but it was good practice, she thought, to keep her mind active. She scanned back over the past twelve months, almost as part of her 80th birthday reflections. She could see when she'd had that rather expensive shopping trip to Dublin; it was lovely to see Pete, although they didn't have the Dublin Racing Festival to go to that time. She could also see when she had cancelled her subscription to that ancestry website, not long after her Park Mill adventure.

She closed the banking page down, but the task had given her pause for thought. It still troubled her that her forebears could have been associated with the mill opposite. Mitsy tried to put it to the back of her mind, as the lunch bell rang.

Sitting next to Anne during lunch, Mitsy asked her what she enjoyed doing in her leisure time. "Now that's a sore topic!" she said and for an instant Misty wished she hadn't asked the question. "You see, I used to spend almost all of my spare time exercising. I ran a ballet class and I attended a friend's yoga sessions, as well as going swimming once a week. Then, really quite suddenly, I realised that my hips and knees didn't want to do those things anymore."

"I'm sorry," said Mitsy, "that must be both disappointing and frustrating?"

"Well, I carried on for a while but everything got too painful."

They sat in silence pondering the unkindness of ageing.

"I do have a new hobby though!" exclaimed Anne, as if she had just thought of it. "I'm into photography now. I can see so many interesting things from my ground floor room so I'm teaching myself to capture shots of birds, when they don't fly off, and flowers when they do."

"Oh," said Mitsy. "You could come to my room if you like, as it looks out directly into the garden. You could watch the birds on the feeder I've put outside my window."

Anne smiled her thanks and said she would enjoy that, maybe some time next week.

Lunch was macaroni cheese and as soon as she had finished hers, Mitsy left the dining room with a new resolve to revitalise her family tree.

Back in room six, in front of her laptop, she did a quick search to see if there were any other websites offering similar access to the ancestry one that she had used before.

She was delighted to find several and picked one that offered the first month free of charge. She signed up, which involved agreeing to pay a modest amount each month. She could see that it was possible to cancel the arrangement before the end of the first four weeks, which appealed to her just in case she decided not to do much more searching into the family tree.

Next, she looked for the notebook she had been using which was tucked away on a bookshelf. She wasn't terribly impressed by the notes she had made previously. Hmmm. I didn't really get far last time, she said to herself. I shall try to be more focussed today. She began with checking her father's details and not surprisingly, given that she already knew them, was able to confirm quite quickly when David Thompson, musician, was born and when he died. She was also happy to find the date when David and Iris were married, although she didn't really remember her parents celebrating their anniversaries the way she and Peter did.

Then she went back to her dad's birth certificate and found that his father was called Herbert and his mother Alice. Herbert was shown as a toolmaker although Mitsy was unable to find out what industry he worked in.

Mitsy was quite weary by this stage, so she decided that some fresh air would help her to concentrate. The walk to the woods that she and Kate first took, so many months ago, immediately came to mind.

Out in the main road, she was able to see that the development work at Park Mill, was almost finished. A large sign heralded the opening of the show home next week, along with claims that several apartments had already been sold. I shall be pleased when they take that ugly fencing down so we can see the façade again, she thought to herself.

The short walk did indeed revive her spirits. She had picked some wild garlic which she hoped might be useful for the kitchen staff. The pretty white flowers were attractive, even if they only used them for garnish. Back home, when she rang the doorbell, Maggie opened the door and smiled to see that some colour had returned to Mitsy's cheeks.

Back at her desk, Mitsy addressed herself to the task with renewed vigour. Her grandfather's name was Herbert Thompson and she wanted to find out more about his father. While she had been out, the website had obligingly identified some possible leads and she worked her way slowly and carefully through the options. She found the Frederick David Thompson that she had spotted some months ago but she also found a plain Frederick Thompson. She realised that she had made an assumption that the former was accurate on the basis that the middle name of David had been handed down the male line. Checking more carefully, the dates of death did not quite tie up. Frederick Thompson, moreover, had lived and worked in Leeds. In the census data, there was no employment information at all, although Mitsy thought that he would have been middle aged at that date.

She went back again to the records for Frederick David Thompson, the overlooker who she had previously guessed was the man in charge at the mill. Again, the website came up trumps by finding some church records which could well have been his burial. Suddenly Mitsy saw what had been staring her in the face right from the outset – that this Frederick David Thompson died at the age of 24 and could not be her great grandfather, and it seemed rather unlikely that he was the overlooker at the mill either.

I suppose it was quite a popular name and I do blame myself for so quickly jumping to a conclusion, she thought.

Rather chastened by the experience, she proceeded to check out the details of the Frederick Thompson from Leeds. He appeared to have a great number of siblings, many of whom did not survive into adulthood. At this point she absolutely drew a blank and was unable to find out anything else, which was disappointing as she had hoped to discover something exciting or interesting.

Mitsy was just wondering whether to persevere when her phone rang. It was Arthur. "'Just wanted to see how you are," he said.

"I'm fine thank you Arthur. I've had a rather trying day working again at my family tree. I suppose one bit of good news is that the man who I thought was my great grandfather isn't and anyway he wasn't an overlooker at the mill."

Arthur was not really sure what Mitsy was talking about but he did have a hazy memory that it was all rather important to his friend at the time of her escapade in the old mill.

"Oh, well I'm glad that it's good news Mitsy. I also wondered if you have heard anything recently from your son Pete?"

"No, I haven't. Oh! There's an email from him. I didn't see it earlier because I was so busy looking at the ancestry stuff. Mmm. He says he is popping over to see me on Saturday, just a quick visit en route to somewhere."

"I just wondered because by some coincidence I had a phone call from Jackie, saying something similar, that she would be calling in on Saturday about midday on her way back from a meeting in Edinburgh."

Mitsy smiled. "Well, I never. That is a coincidence!"

"And the other reason I was phoning you Mitsy, is that I was going to suggest that next Wednesday, we call in to look at the new apartments across the road before we have our lunchtime session at the Standsfield?"

"Would we be allowed? I mean, if we have no intention of buying one?" she giggled.

"I won't tell them if you don't! It's a date then! See you soon. And don't be spending too long working at that computer of yours while the weather is lovely." With that he rang off, leaving Mitsy to ponder all manner of things.

27

Today's outing for the Appledore House residents was billed as a 'magical mystery tour', although Mitsy privately suspected that the minibus driver would just meander around wherever he pleased. Yes, that probably was a little unkind but as it turned out, not far off the mark.

First, they headed straight into the city centre, which was rather busy as it was full of Friday morning shoppers. Sally was with them as the responsible member of staff. She was relatively new to Bradford so the assembled group were only too happy to point out landmarks.

They bombarded her with information:

"See, that's the Alhambra! It's a beautiful building. It's a theatre and they have all sorts of plays on there. And the Christmas panto – don't forget the panto!"

Mitsy mentioned to Raymond, who was sitting next to her, that the National Museum of Photography, Film and Television was supposed to be worth a visit. She pointed it out as they drove past. "Oh look. That couple holding hands going into the museum, don't they look ever so much like my son Pete and Arthur's daughter Jackie?" She said it out loud and wondered afterwards whether people would always think of her as the woman who saw imaginary things.

As they drove round the busy streets, there was much discussion by the passengers as to which curry house was the best. Mitsy favoured the Kashmir, which is one of the oldest in the city. She and Peter used to go there quite often. The restaurant doesn't have a license to sell alcohol but you were allowed to take your own bottle in and just pay corkage.

Soon, the minibus was heading away from the city and passing through Shipley, Keighley and Ilkley. En route, the passengers were still pointing out the sights to Sally. The driver parked at the Cow and Calf Rocks viewpoint up on Ilkley Moor and everyone got out for a breath of fresh air and for some of them to take photos.

Finally, to complete their outing, the minibus took them to the market town of Otley and then back to Appledore House. All in all, it was a pleasant tour and everyone thanked the driver as they descended the vehicle.

Mitsy generally opted for these trips even though she knew the places well, because it made a change from sitting in her room. She also appreciated the fact that someone else was doing the driving.

28

Mitsy woke early on Saturday, partly because she was looking forward to seeing her son Pete, and partly because the sun was shining straight into her face. Every day, someone came to clean and dust her room in the morning and as she was right at the far end of the corridor, they usually began with room six. It helped that everyone knew she was an early riser. Today it was Sally, who had accompanied them on their outing the day before.

Sally vacuumed very efficiently and then cleaned and disinfected the bathroom before finishing off with polish on the furniture in the living area. When Mitsy first moved into Appledore House she was quite embarrassed to have someone clean for her but over time she had got used to it. Sally also changed the towels today and on Monday the bed linen would be changed too. It all went off in a big van to a laundry in the centre of Bradford and was returned three days later fresh, clean, aired and ironed.

Mitsy and Sally talked about the previous day's drive and the surprise birthday party on Wednesday. Mitsy also mentioned that her son was calling in to see her later today. These little conversations were of no real importance but, as Mitsy was astute enough to recognise, they were important in terms of a person's mental wellbeing. Had she still been living on her own, she may not have had an opportunity to talk to another person for several days on end.

As it turned out, she didn't have to wait long, as Pete arrived just in time for coffee.

They sat and chatted about all sorts of things and Pete mentioned that he would like to take Mitsy out for lunch to the Stansfield Arms. She noticed that he kept looking at his watch, which was unusual as he didn't generally worry about time. In fact, he had a tendency to be late, even when it was important. At twenty to twelve he suggested his mother should get ready to go out, so they could have a leisurely walk to the pub.

Mitsy was already wearing a smart trouser suit so she didn't see the need to change. To please Pete, she brushed her hair, put on just a little make-up and finished off with perfume.

"Will I do?" she asked, twirling in front of him.

"Yes, mother. You look lovely!"

Mitsy noticed that Pete was wearing aftershave and in fact had made quite an effort with his appearance himself.

They walked past the rental car Pete had hired and strolled comfortably together along the level path to the pub.

At the door, Patsy the landlady came out: "Ah Mr Howard, your table is in the dining room and your guests have arrived already."

Mitsy looked at Pete whose expression was annoyingly blank so she couldn't figure out what was happening.

"I know you usually eat in the bar, but I thought it would be nice to sit in the restaurant today, especially as we have guests," he said to his mum.

As they crossed the threshold of the restaurant, Mitsy was delighted to see Arthur waving to her and Jackie sitting next to her father.

"Well, fancy seeing you here!" she exclaimed, somewhat unoriginally.

Pete moved back a chair for his mother to sit down while commenting, "We have some news to share with you."

Jackie smiled at Mitsy. "Good morning, Mrs Howard. How are you today?"

Mitsy smiled and nodded, waiting for some announcement.

"We wanted to tell you both together," said Pete.

"We're getting engaged!" the happy pair chorused.

Amid the cacophony of congratulations and laughter, Patsy walked in carrying a bottle and an ice bucket. "This is on the house. When your son and your daughter booked the table, someone let slip that it was a happy occasion. We do enjoy seeing Arthur and Mitsy on Wednesdays here and the Standsfield Arms wishes everyone all the very best."

After she had left the room, with their thanks ringing in her ears, Mitsy exclaimed, "My goodness, bubbly twice in one week! I could get used to this!"

Pete opened the bottle and proposed a toast to his wife-to-be and then to their parents, thanking them for unwittingly bringing them together.

Conversation paused while they chose from the menu, with three of them choosing roast beef and Jackie going for the vegetarian option.

Once selected, Mitsy decided to cut to the chase. "So.... how did all this happen and what are your plans?"

Jackie explained that they met by chance at the Travelodge when both were visiting their parent. Of course, Mitsy and Arthur were well aware of this, but let the couple continue.

"By good chance," said Pete, "I mentioned to Jackie about grandad's recordings and it turned out that she is a specialist in this field."

"Yes," said Jackie. "It's been so interesting! Your father, Mrs Howard, was well-known in his time. He wrote the incidental music for quite a number of radio shows, although he was often not credited. One of the recordings that Pete showed me was for a comedy programme called, "You Don't Say..." and it is the only copy in existence. Of course, his music for the film "Fire Over England" was really important and was the backdrop to the action which showcased the early work of Laurence Olivier, Flora Robson, Vivien Leigh and Raymond Massey."

Pete carried on, "Anyway, I needed to see Jackie with some more of the tapes and recordings – well, actually it was a good excuse for me to see her again – and we realised how much we enjoyed each other's company."

"And how is this going to work, with one of you in London and the other in Dublin? Not wishing to pour cold water on your happiness," said Arthur, ever the practical one.

"Actually, it has worked out better than we could have hoped," said Jackie. "We have had several months of commuting back and forth to see each other, so there's been time to think it through carefully. Where I work has been having a reorganisation and I volunteered to be one of the people who works from home in future. I shall be living with Pete in Dublin for three weeks each month and I will be in my London flat for three or four days of the remaining week. This means I can meet with colleagues, collect materials and then head back to my main home with Pete the rest of the time. It also means that if Pete needs a London stop-over at any time, he can use my place."

Privately, Mitsy thought that this arrangement would prove rather expensive over time because running two homes in two busy, and expensive, cities seemed an extravagance. However, she held her tongue because they seemed so delighted to have found a solution to a long-distance relationship for now. In the future, she hoped to tactfully share some of her own experience with them both. After all, maintaining a long and happy relationship with one's partner away at sea had taken some doing as she knew all too well.

By this stage of the explanations, the meals had arrived so everyone concentrated on eating while making comments on the happy news.

The remainder of the champagne was finished off by the older couple, as Pete and Jackie had a short drive and a flight before getting home. "Thank you both for your consideration in telling us together," said Arthur. "I don't think either of us would have been able to keep it a secret from the other."

Jackie looked at her watch, and nodded to Pete who excused himself as if he was heading to the gents. As it happened, he went to pay the bill, as discretely as possible. On his return, he smiled and said, "I suggest you two sit and have a coffee to finish off your meal, while we head for the airport. I'm sorry it's a flying visit but we both have quite a busy schedule next week."

"Oh," said Jackie. "I know what else I meant to say. First, I hope that when you next come over for a shopping trip Mrs Howard that I can join you. You can bring Dad if you like, although I'm not sure it's his scene! Also, we haven't made any wedding plans yet. Pete's proposal was all quite sudden and we wanted to tell you first."

"That sounds good to me," said Mitsy, "with one proviso. Please call me Mitsy! I shall enjoy shopping with you too."

Mitsy and Arthur kissed and hugged their offspring as the pair dashed off for the journey home.

"Well," said Mitsy to Arthur, after they had left. "I think we both had a suspicion about their developing friendship but I had no idea it had progressed this far. I'm so happy for them. I thought my Pete would remain a bachelor for the rest of his life and I do know he's quite choosy, so this is great news. I hope it works out for them."

"I'm fairly confident it will," said Arthur, "and Jackie may not have chosen so well for her first marriage but she's older and wiser now. It's great news!"

"As ever, the Standsfield has done us proud. Now let's have some coffee."

29

The early part of the week flew by, with Mitsy only going out to the post office to buy a congratulations card for Pete and Jackie. She thought it would be something for them to keep as a memento of this happy time. She asked Arthur to sign it too as she assumed, correctly, that it wouldn't have occurred to him to get a card.

Mitsy was noticing that she had far fewer sleepless nights the longer she lived at Appledore House. It may have been something to do with having fully settled in to the Care Home or just that she had fewer things to worry about now. Of course, with that very ugly high fence around the housing development, there wasn't much for her to see at night.

On Tuesday, the hated fence was taken down and a couple of trucks took the sections away. Mitsy was a little surprised that the building looked much the same as it did before the works started. Obviously, one or two important changes were in evidence, such as the sapling that had been growing out of the mill chimney had been removed and she was guessing that the structure had been capped so it didn't happen again.

She was looking forward to seeing round the interior of Park Mill with Arthur the next day. She remembered very clearly what she saw on her nocturnal visit that night a year ago and she was keen to see if she could recognise anything.

When the day arrived, she made sure to dress smartly, although she was well aware that people lived in jeans or track suits these days and no one thought any the less of them. Still, I prefer to keep up my standards, she said to herself.

Meeting up with Arthur by the front door of Appledore House, Mitsy's excitement was obvious. She was hopping from foot to foot and an enormous grin adorned her happy face. "Now then, my dear Mitsy, I don't want to raise your expectations because the new apartments may be quite a disappointment you know."

They walked across the road, with Arthur trying to keep Mitsy in check. "Stop rushing!" he admonished.

An estate agency had set up the Open House event and quite a few people were lurking outside the impressive portico for the temporary office to open.

Finally, two very smart young women in corporate navy suits appeared, unlocked the door and gestured for people to go in. One of the apartments had been fully furnished, in order to give an impression of what it would be like to live there. A corner of the spacious living room had a desk in the corner with leaflets and information sheets.

It was clear that one of the women would be taking on greeting duties and the other was there to show people round.

Arthur and Mitsy followed the crowd, looking in every room and making quiet comments to each other. What was immediately obvious was that each apartment was very modern and did not in any way reflect the age of the original building.

They exchanged glances as the guide extolled the virtues of all the integrated kitchen appliances. It was difficult to feign much interest because living at Appledore House meant that those things were someone else's worry!

The bathroom was well equipped, much like Mitsy's bathroom at Appledore House, although here it was attractively decorated with mirror glass tiles. Mitsy couldn't help wondering how that worked out when one wandered in, all bleary-eyed of a morning. Imagine seeing multiple versions of oneself undressed and half-awake!

The bedrooms were fine, all attractively colour co-ordinated. The lounge had an enormous television, again they presumed to show potential buyers what a luxury apartment could offer.

Mitsy found it difficult to see where the main room of the former mill had been, as she remembered it. There was no sign of the high ceiling or, of course, the looms, the machines or where the cotton bales stood. She concluded that much of the interior of each apartment had been pre-fabricated and installed inside the outer shell of the building.

"Excuse me," asked Mitsy, bravely, "these apartments do have parking, don't they?"

"Oh yes. Every property has a numbered space and there are parking lots for guests. The concierge will ensure that only residents park here."

Of course, that wasn't quite what Mitsy wanted to know, but she persevered: "and how do we access them?"

The young woman was all too happy to show Mitsy and Arthur the way to the corridor that led outside. "Please come back this way so that we can answer any questions that you or your husband still have."

Mitsy and Arthur grinned at each other being described as husband and wife and headed off down the corridor.

"Oh yes, this is how I remember it. All those rooms in there were the recent additions but this is the way I came in."

Soon, they were at the back door which led them out to the parking area as described. As well as the parking bays, all numbered they presumed to tie up with the apartment numbers, there was a small sitting area with an ornamental tree. "I suppose they've made the best of a small space," said Arthur.

"Do we go back in?"

"I don't think so, Mitsy. If we're not careful they will be signing us up to buy one! That is, of course, if you've seen enough?"

As they walked steadily towards the Standsfield Arms, laughing and making general observations about the modern layout of the properties, Mitsy became thoughtful.

"You know, Arthur, I could see how the building had been the mill I saw, and I recognised the shared areas like the portico entrance hall and the corridor going out to the car park, but actually I couldn't "feel" the presence of the people I saw. I cannot explain it better than that, other than to say it all felt blank and empty."

"Do you think perhaps that this visit to Park Mill has given you, what they call in modern parlance "closure"?

Misty nodded thoughtfully and recognised what a good and kind friend Arthur was.

"I've also been thinking..."

"Whoa, don't overdo the thinking Mitsy!" said Arthur playfully.

"Yes, I've been thinking that seeing the White Lady and the people working in the mill was all part of my adjustment to a major life change. I was very stressed and quite afraid of making the move to a Care Home. I think that made me hypersensitive to the emotions of others, even those who only remained in spirit form. Does that sound silly?"

"Not at all. It's only natural that we feel uncomfortable with life changes like that. I think perhaps you were seeking to find associations within your new home area. I mean, look at me, I spent hours looking into the history of Appledore House, for much the same reasons."

They arrived at the pub and Mitsy gave Arthur a hug. "Thank you for being such an understanding friend."

"My pleasure, madam," said Arthur, as he made a bow as if to an imaginary royal personage.

A small portion of fish and chips was ordered for each of them as they sat in their usual corner of the bar. Peter the dog ambled in, accepted a pat and curled himself up on the rug even thought the fire was not lit.

"So, just to conclude Arthur, I have decided not to do anymore ancestor hunting. It was a good idea after my husband died as it gave me something to focus on. It was useful for the family at the outset as it gave us evidence of our Irish heritage for Pete to settle in Dublin. I'm not sure it serves a purpose now."

"You know what I think? That programme on the telly has a lot to answer for!"

"What programme?"

"I think it's called 'Who Do You Think You Are?' They have a celebrity who is taken all over the place for example, to the USA, Ireland, Australia or Germany and they show them things about their forebears. It's quite thought-provoking and entertaining but it does give the impression that anyone can do this. In reality the BBC has a team of researchers working for months before they film the episode and only then when they have a good tale to tell!"

"Well, you could be right Arthur. Anyway, I'm leaving it alone for good!"

After they had enjoyed their fish and chips, Mitsy looked at her watch.

"It's been a lovely morning Arthur, and now I must dash because I have someone phoning me this afternoon after two-thirty. Can we head back now, if that's OK?"

Arthur was intrigued but did not like to ask about the phone call as it was probably something private like a solicitor. From what he knew of Mitsy's sister Sky, it wasn't likely to be her, he thought!

Grabbing her door key inside Appledore House, Mitsy hurried off with a friendly farewell and "See you tomorrow."

30

The next morning, three people received somewhat mysterious text messages from their friend Mitsy. All it said was:

Please meet me in the garden at 15:00. Tea and chocolate biscuits provided! ☺

At ten to three - which was early because none of them could wait - Arthur, Norma and Kate assembled in the garden. There was a small table with a flowery table cloth and four chairs set out as if it was waiting for them. Having questioned each other on the purpose of their meeting and with no-one any the wiser, they sat down to wait.

Jo appeared with a tray of cups, saucers, a milk jug and a full teapot but she had no idea what it was all about either.

Mitsy could see her friends arrive from her bedroom window which was overlooking the garden but she wanted to wait until the moment was right. Eventually, she emerged herself, carrying a plate of biscuits.

"Well this is lovely; we should do this more often!" said Kate.

Mitsy smiled. "I'm happy with that, especially if we have tea in the garden every occasion I have a book published!!"

The group exploded with comments until Mitsy patted the air to ask them to stop.

"I'm sure you are all aware that I have been writing a book for some months. Yesterday I had a phone call from someone who I can now call 'my publisher'!"

Mitsy poured out the tea and handed round the biscuits while everyone congratulated her and exclaimed how lovely it was to have a real author in their midst.

"What is it about?" asked Norma.

"What's it called?" asked Kate.

"How soon will it go into print?" asked Arthur

"Ha-ha, only one question at a time," said Mitsy. "It won't be published for a while, as I still have to do the final editing. Then I'll be choosing the cover and writing all the bits and pieces such as crediting those who helped and the dedication.

"It's called *Violet's Story* and I have Arthur to thank for that. It's a novel based on some of the history of this house and what happened when it was a Red Cross Hospital. Most of it is entirely fictitious."

The little group carried on chatting for a while and Mitsy thought how wonderful it was, to achieve something new at her age. She also realised that she was very happy here, amongst friends. Life was good.

If you enjoyed reading *The Enduring Curiosity of Mitsy Howard - A Walk in the Mill,* I would be delighted if you would write a short review for me. You can do this on https://www.amazon.co.uk.

Reviews are very important for authors, as well as for anyone wondering whether to order a book, so any way in which you can help is much appreciated!

I have written four other books, all of which are available via Amazon or to order through any good bookseller. My books are held in the British Library and in selected local libraries. They are available in both paperback format and e-book editions. Further information on the books can be found on the following pages.

You can also checkout my Facebook author page www.facebook.com/carolesusansmith which provides news, updates and information about current activities.

If you would like to send me any comments, feedback or criticism you can message me on the Facebook page or send an email to carolesusansmith@pnwriter.org I love to hear from readers!

TravelWorks by Carole Susan Smith

From the age of nineteen Carole decided that travelling to other countries was a lot of fun. She realised that she would need time and money to do more of this. Discovering that the nine-to-five life was definitely not for her, she decided to look for jobs that paid her to travel while working.

Some of her travels have been to places that others might not choose for a holiday or even a short break. Some places, such as Siberia in mid-winter and the Middle East in the height of summer, were encountered in the least propitious circumstances and seasons.

Her fascinating adventures over the last forty years reflect changes in politics and society as well as in travel itself.

This book of stories, diaries and reflections is for fellow travellers and armchair travellers alike who will appreciate that travel is education and entertainment wrapped up in a colourful package.

HomeWorks by Carole Susan Smith

Carole's first book took the reader to Yekaterinburg, Gaza City, Goteborg and Taipei with various other destinations in between. Whilst Southampton, Manchester, Bristol, Glasgow, Caernarfon, London and Leeds are not as obviously exotic, you may be surprised by some of her adventures nearer to home.

As you accompany Carole on her journeys you will discover why packing a torch on a business trip can get you into trouble and how a jacuzzi makes a good meeting room. Spending time with oil executives speaking six different languages poses no problems for her but trying to understand their technical language does. You may wonder why ninety men were determined to address her as Your Majesty or how come she was standing on a desk quoting Middle English.

Her excuse is that she's never been afraid to try something different but you will have to read the whole book to make sense of this!

Oh, and another thing... by Carole Susan Smith

Whether you are applying for a job or in conversation with someone you don't know well, sooner or later you will be asked about your hobbies and interests. Having penned two books about travelling and work life, I thought I should complete the trilogy by confessing to some of the slightly odd things I have done in my leisure time.

These include cycling, which didn't end well: "What was intended to be a stylish wheelie manoeuvre across the loose gravel turned into more of a flying circus demonstration".

You will also discover much about outdoor exploits, including caving, climbing and long-distance walking.

In ***Oh, and another thing...*** you will have another opportunity to read a light-hearted book about all the other things I forgot to tell you in ***TravelWorks*** and ***HomeWorks!***

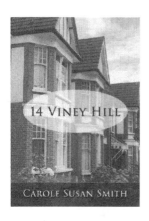

14 Viney Hill by Carole Susan Smith

After a rocky start in life, Jane Bonneville thought she had everything sorted. A gorgeous husband and a safe, loving and stable home for their children. Totally opposite to her own childhood.

It was all going rather well until her world turned upside down one Friday in March...

Printed in Great Britain
by Amazon

21342891R00088